"I've decided to get married."

Caitlin felt the blood leave her face. Why did she feel so shocked—so betrayed? She swallowed hard. Alec was her friend. If he'd fallen in love—found a woman to marry—she ought to feel happy for him.

"Congratulations," she said, injecting as much zing into her voice as she possibly could. "I'm so pleased for you, Alec. Who is ... who is the lucky woman?"

Alec smiled cheerfully. "I've no idea. Not yet."

Caitlin stared at him blankly. "What on earth do you mean? How can you decide to get married without knowing who you want for your wife?"

"Easily," he said. "With your help. You're my best friend, you've known me for years, plus you've got loads of experience interviewing job applicants. I'm counting on *you* to find the right woman for me."

Jasmine Cresswell's writing career began when she finally decided to stop writing research papers and try her hand at a novel. It was obviously the right choice! Born in England, Jasmine has lived and worked all over the world. She met her husband, another expatriate Britisher, in Rio de Janeiro. They're currently living in Florida. Jasmine is the mother of three daughters and one son, who are all "amazingly tolerant" of her addiction to writing.

Books by Jasmine Cresswell

Don't miss any of our special offers. Write to us at the following address for information on our newest releases.

Harlequin Reader Service
P.O. Box 1397, Buffalo, NY 14240
Canadian address: P.O. Box 603,
Fort Erie, Ont. L2A 5X3

THE PERFECT BRIDE
Jasmine Cresswell

Harlequin Books

TORONTO • NEW YORK • LONDON
AMSTERDAM • PARIS • SYDNEY • HAMBURG
STOCKHOLM • ATHENS • TOKYO • MILAN
MADRID • WARSAW • BUDAPEST • AUCKLAND

ISBN 0-373-03270-6

Harlequin Romance first edition June 1993

THE PERFECT BRIDE

CHAPTER ONE

SAM ALWAYS CHOSE five-thirty Friday afternoon to throw a tantrum. The staff at Services Unlimited had grown accustomed to having their weekends kicked off by Sam hyperventilating over some crisis or other. This time, unfortunately, Sam had decided to stage his weekly scene over one of Caitlin's projects.

He stormed into her office, looking as threatening as a man can look when he's chubby, five foot four and blessed with no more than a dozen silvery hairs carefully arranged over his bald pink scalp.

He shook a fistful of papers under Caitlin's nose. "This reference from the Countess of Yardleigh stinks. How come you're still recommending this Tittleswit guy for the job? Why didn't you recommend Jackson? Jackson is already in Washington, and he's got a slew of solid American references."

Caitlin drew a deep breath and managed a reassuring smile. She loved her job, her colleagues and her life in general. Most days, she even loved her boss, Sam Bergen. This afternoon, however, she admitted to feeling frazzled. It had already been a long tough week. "The man's name is Littlethwaite, Sam. Algernon Littlethwaite. Not Tittleswit."

"Yeah, and his references stink."

"Sam, I called the Countess of Yardleigh and spoke to her in person for twenty minutes. She thinks Algernon Littlethwaite is an excellent butler, but she's very restrained and uppercrust British. Her definition of lavish praise is to say that Algernon 'fulfilled his duties to the best of his ability.' Don't worry, Sam, we've found the perfect butler for the Japanese ambassador.''

Sam had no intention of being mollified. Late on Fridays, he seemed to enjoy worrying. ''What about Littlethwaite's work permits? God knows what kind of runaround they'll give you at Immigration if his paperwork isn't in order.''

Caitlin reminded herself that she was paid an excellent salary and that the job market in Washington, DC, was tight. ''As you can see if you've read the file, Sam, Mr. Littlethwaite faxed us copies of his visas and documentation three weeks ago. He has absolutely everything he could possibly need to work legally in this country, and I'm sure he'll arrive from London tomorrow afternoon right on schedule.''

A tap on the door of her office was followed by the immediate entry of Dot, her secretary. ''Sorry to interrupt, Sam, but Caitlin has to sign these letters right away if we want them to catch tonight's mail. As it is, I'll have to take them to the late pickup box.''

Caitlin flashed her secretary a grateful smile. ''Sorry, Sam, but I really must read these through before I sign them.''

Sam left Caitlin's office, gloomily predicting that Mr. Littlethwaite would turn out to be a con man and that Services Unlimited would be dragged into bankruptcy as Sam valiantly tried to fend off lawsuits from the disgruntled Japanese ambassador.

Dot shook her head. ''What is it about Friday nights?'' she asked. ''From Monday morning until quitting time on Friday, Sam Bergen is an intelligent, considerate, efficient employer. The clock strikes five on Friday and suddenly he grows fangs and turns into a monster.''

''I think he misses his wife. Friday nights used to be special for them. It was the only time he absolutely refused to allow business to intrude. Now he has nothing to look forward to except an empty house and a lonely weekend.''

''Poor man, but Shirley's been dead for two years now. He should get out and about more. Find himself a nice woman to liven up his lonely weekends.''

Caitlin finished signing letters and handed the bulging folder back to her secretary. ''Dot, I left home so that I wouldn't be surrounded by people who think getting married is the cure for all the world's problems. Don't you start, please.''

Dot held up her hands in protest. ''Caitlin, honey, I never said one single word about Sam needing a wife. I said he needed a nice woman he could date, that's all. I'm no fan of matrimony.''

''Sure. That's why you've been married three times.''

''Right, and divorced twice and widowed once. It's taken me twenty years, but I finally got smart. From now on, the men in my life are gonna be strictly short-term and strictly by appointment. Marriage is a one-way street, with all the advantages going in the man's direction.''

''You're too cynical,'' Caitlin said, although in her heart of hearts she didn't really disagree with her secretary.

''Wait until you're married—then we'll have this conversation again.''

"We'll have to wait a long time. I'm not planning to get married for the next hundred years or so."

"Huh, you're too pretty to stay that smart. Chestnut hair, green eyes, curves in all the right places. Honey, you're a surefire bride-in-waiting if ever I saw one." Dot grabbed her jacket and purse, tucked the package of mail under her arm and waved from the doorway. "See you on Monday, boss. Have a good weekend. And if you're seeing that gorgeous hunk Alec Woodward tonight, give him a kiss from me."

"Gorgeous hunk? *Alec?*"

Dot shot her a curious glance. "In case you haven't noticed, honey, he's endowed with one heck of a body hidden under those conservative lawyer's suits of his. Not to mention that he has a pair of wicked blue eyes, expressly designed to make any normal woman sit up and beg for attention. If you're determined to stay single, I recommend you keep away from Alec Woodward."

Caitlin chuckled in genuine amusement. "I'm not in the least danger, Dot, I promise you. Alec and I don't think of each other that way."

"You're not blind, girl. How can you avoid thinking of him that way?"

"Easily, because he's my friend. Alec moved in next door when I was eight. That means I've known him for twenty years, and in all that time, I can honestly say I've never noticed his wicked blue eyes. So I don't suppose they're going to start driving me insane with longing any time soon, do you?"

"Keep it that way, hon, and you'll live a happy life. Lovers and husbands are two a penny. Good friends are a heck of a lot harder to find. Especially of the male variety." She shrugged, gazing at Caitlin thoughtfully.

"Of course, if a woman ever did manage to find a lover who was also a friend, then I guess she'd have a match made in heaven."

Caitlin grimaced. "Don't hold your breath."

"Honey, I've lived long enough to know that anything can happen in this world. Sometimes even the good things. Have a nice weekend." Whistling under her breath, Dot ran for the elevator.

Relieved of the secretary's cheerful presence, the office suddenly seemed so quiet as to be oppressive. Thank heaven it was Friday, Caitlin thought, as she tidied away the papers for her newest client. It was good to know that her hard work had paid off and that she personally had filled three important positions during the past week. In addition to Mr. Littlethwaite, she'd found a housekeeper for the chairman of the World Bank and a sous-chef for the White House, but she'd worked too many fourteen-hour days recently, and she desperately needed a break.

Perhaps she'd call Alec and see if he could join her for a drink after work. Or, better yet, they could spend the entire evening together. They could have a pizza at Mama Maria's, the Italian restaurant they'd discovered a few months ago, and then catch the late show at one of the nearby movie theaters.

Talking to Dot had reminded her it must be more than two weeks since she'd seen Alec. Now that she stopped to think about him, Caitlin realized she'd missed Alec a lot. In fact, she was surprised how much she hoped he hadn't already made a hot date with one of the luscious female law students who swarmed around his office.

She stopped filing papers and reached for the phone, but before she could dial the number for Alec's office, her other line buzzed. She almost didn't answer the call, then discipline won out over personal feelings. She switched lines and responded politely.

"Hello, this is Caitlin Howard."

"Oh, Lin, can you believe it? I'm pregnant! The doctor confirmed it this afternoon. He says I'm seven weeks pregnant and everything's fine. Jeff and I are so happy we're practically swinging from the chandeliers. Or we would be, if we had any chandeliers."

Her sister's excitement fizzed and bubbled over the miles of fiber-optic cable. Caitlin experienced the oddest little lurch in the pit of her stomach. It was a second or two before she managed to reply, and her sister's voice came again, more tentatively.

"Hey, Lin, are you still there?"

Caitlin shook off a wave of sudden, inexplicable exhaustion. "Yes, I'm here. Merry, that's wonderful news. Congratulations! I'm so pleased for you and Jeff. I know how much you both wanted to start a family. It's going to be a first grandchild for Jeff's parents, isn't it?"

"Yes, they're almost as thrilled as we are. After two years and no success, we were beginning to wonder if I'd ever get pregnant!" Merry giggled. "And it sure wasn't for want of trying, believe me. Jeff and I really worked at this project! Gosh, this is the most exciting day of our lives. We're driving into Youngstown this weekend to look at cribs and to buy curtains for the nursery. Megan and George are coming, too, but they're leaving the boys with Mom and Dad—you know how carsick they get."

"I sure do," Caitlin said with feeling, remembering a disastrous outing at Christmas when she had been responsible for entertaining her two young nephews, Zach and Matt, the sons of her other sister, Megan. She'd learned the hard way that toddlers of two and three can't consume hot dogs followed by ice cream followed by popcorn and then drive home in the back of a station wagon without disastrous consequences.

Merry laughed sympathetically. "You're so smart, Lin, but I swear you don't have an ounce of common sense. I don't know how you manage to run that agency of yours when you only need to *look* at a vacuum cleaner to have it break down."

Caitlin had long ago given up trying to convince her family that providing trained domestic help for the ambassadors, senators and other dignitaries of the nation's capital did not require her to run out and personally dust furniture. "So when is this special baby due exactly? Sometime next spring?" she asked. "I'll have to be sure to save some vacation time for visiting with my new niece or nephew."

"May fifteenth, can you believe it? Wouldn't it be wonderful if our baby arrived right on your birthday?"

"The best present I could have," Caitlin said. "And I plan to lobby hard to be chosen as one of the godparents."

"You're already chosen. Jeff and I couldn't think of anyone we love more, even though we don't understand you." Merry's cheerful voice became somewhat wistful. "Megan and I were talking about how the baby's due on your birthday and all. Do you realize you're going to be twenty-nine next May, which is only one year away from being thirty? Gosh, Lin, aren't you worried?"

"What about?" Caitlin asked, although she knew very well what her sister was trying to say. "Last time I checked with the dentist, she assured me my teeth aren't going to fall out any time soon. And the doctor seems to think I can hold off on ordering my wheelchair for at least another five years, maybe even ten.''

Merry refused to be diverted. "You know that isn't what I mean. It's not your health we're worried about— it's the fact that you're still single. With all those glamorous men in Washington, Megan and I can't understand why you haven't managed to get yourself settled yet. Haven't you met any exciting men recently?''

Merry sounded almost pleading, and Caitlin resisted the impulse to snap at her youngest sister. She forced a laugh. "Sure, I met this marvelous English butler, who wears starched wing collars and is called Algernon Littlethwaite. I didn't believe there were people outside TV sitcoms who had names like that, did you?''

"Caitlin, don't joke. I meant have you met any *eligible* men. Men you've gone out with on a date. Men you might want to marry.''

Caitlin sighed. She knew from long experience of dealing with Merry—not to mention the rest of her family—that it would prove quicker and easier to tell her what she wanted to hear. Nobody in Caitlin's family was prepared to believe the simple truth: that Caitlin had no particular desire to get married, that she liked her life and her career just the way they were.

"I had dinner with a congressman from Kentucky a couple of weeks ago,'' she said. "He's very good-looking and very sincere about wanting to improve government funding for rural education. You know how strongly I feel about that, so we had a lot in common.''

Merry, who had a low opinion of politicians, seemed unimpressed by the congressman from Kentucky. "Anyone else?" she asked.

"Last weekend I went sailing with one of the assistant curators at the Smithsonian. He was very nice. He's a graduate of Georgetown University, five years before me, so we had lots to talk about."

"What's his name?

"David."

"Did you really like him?" Merry couldn't conceal her eagerness, or the faint undertone of anxiety. "I mean are you going to see him again soon?"

"I hope so," Caitlin said lightly. "But I wouldn't start making any wedding plans for another decade or two."

"Gosh, Lin, you're so hard to please. Who are you waiting for, for heaven's sake? Prince Charming? Superman?"

"I'm not that picky. Any millionaire who looks like Mel Gibson and has the soul of a poet could capture my heart in a minute."

"You always joke about it, Lin, but it's not a joking matter. What's going to happen ten years from now when you're president of Services Unlimited but all alone in your fancy Washington apartment, and the only person who calls on Saturday night is a client complaining that the chef you sent around to the embassy doesn't know how to cook frogs' legs, or toads' knees or whatever gross thing they're eating in Washington that month."

It had been a long day on top of a *very* long week. Caitlin tried hard not to feel angry with her sister. Merry never meant to pry, or to intrude, or to push her own values onto Caitlin. The trouble was, Merry and Megan were throwbacks to the fifties who couldn't believe that any woman was truly happy until she was married. Caitlin's enthusiasm for working hard at a demanding job in a huge city like Washington, DC, struck her sisters as both inexplicable and sad. They had been on a nonstop, five-year campaign to get Caitlin married and comfortably "settled down," preferably in their hometown of Hapsburg, Ohio.

"You know, Lin," Merry went on, "if you were honest with yourself, you'd admit that a woman's never really fulfilled until she has a home and a husband of her own."

Caitlin's self-control snapped. She was on the verge of saying something she probably would have regretted for years when a familiar friendly face appeared in the doorway.

She sprang from her chair, dropping the phone onto her desk. "Alec, oh, thank heaven you're here!"

Alec's casual smile hardened, just for an instant, into an expression Caitlin found unreadable. Which was odd, because she usually knew exactly what Alec was thinking. Over the years, they'd grown to understand each other so well that sometimes they were like an old married couple, communicating in jumbled half sentences and vague gestures.

"Alec?" she said uncertainly.

The split second of tension vanished, and his smile resumed its usual teasing form. "I should stay away more often. It's great to receive such a welcome."

"It must be telepathy," she said. "I was going to call. Boy, am I happy to see you." She retrieved the phone and apologized to her sister. "Sorry, Merry, someone just arrived unexpectedly in my office and I dropped the phone. Clumsy of me. What were we talking about?"

"As if you didn't know." Now it was Merry's turn to sigh. "I suppose this unexpected visitor is another of your important clients, and now you'll waste the weekend locked up in your apartment writing a presentation for him."

It was late and Caitlin was tired. She couldn't think of any other excuse for the imp of mischief that seized her. "Heavens, no, this isn't a client," she said. "It's a hot date." She gave Alec a conspiratorial wink, while Merry spluttered into the phone.

"Oh, great! What's he like?"

"Well, let's see, how should I describe him?" Caitlin pretended to consider her sister's question. "He's thirty-five, he's intelligent and very successful in his career. He also has a great body and wicked blue eyes that would make any woman sit up and beg to be noticed."

"I can't believe what I'm hearing. Caitlin, is this really you talking? And is he still there? Can he hear what you're saying?"

"Yes, he's listening to every word. I think he's stunned by what I just said about his sexy blue eyes. But heck, this is the nineties. Why shouldn't I let him know I think he's attractive?"

Alec leaned against the doorjamb, his much-discussed eyes dancing with laughter, but his expression somewhat quizzical. "Twenty years, and I never knew you cared," he murmured. "Tell me more about my great body."

She grinned, covering the mouthpiece of the phone. "Don't you wish." She uncovered the phone. "Merry, I hate to cut you off, but my date is waiting, and he's such a dynamic man he hates to hang around doing nothing. I'll talk to you later, okay? Tell Jeff congratulations on becoming an expectant father, and good luck with the crib hunt.''

"You know what, Lin, you sound really strange. All sort of discombobulated. Oh, boy, I can't wait to tell Megan. I think maybe you've met the right man at last."

She should have denied it at once, but Caitlin wasn't in the mood to fight a losing battle. She glanced at Alec, inviting him to share the joke. "You're right, Merry. He's far and away the most attractive man I've ever dated. In fact, I don't think I'll ever find another man to compare with him." She said goodbye quickly and hung up the phone, feeling a smidgen of guilt for having deceived her sister.

Alec pushed himself away from the doorjamb and crossed the room to give her a brotherly hug. "What was that all about? I assume it was Merry on the phone."

"It was. And she was so desperate for me to have a date tonight, I transformed you into my hot new prospect for a romantic evening."

"Well, you can't lie to your sister, so I'd better *be* your date for the night. Would you like to go out for a pizza?"

She smiled, not at all surprised that their thoughts were running in harmony. "Great idea. Mama Maria's?"

"Definitely. The house special. Double cheese, no onions, no anchovies."

"Cappuccino coffee with dessert?"

"Mmm...sounds good. You've booked yourself one sizzling date, lady. Let me tell you, I can't wait to hear some more about my great body and wicked blue eyes."

"Wish I could oblige, but there's nothing to add."
She grabbed her purse and, with the ease of long
friendship, hooked her arm through Alec's. "Those
aren't actually my own opinions. I borrowed them from
Dot."

"Your secretary? Hah! I always knew she was a
woman of outstanding perception."

Caitlin laughed. "She's a fantastic typist, too. A
hundred words a minute." She yawned, resting against
the wall as they waited for the elevator. "Whew!" she
said. "You arrived just in the nick of time. Merry was
doing her usual job of putting me through the wringer."

"Is that why she called? To give you a hard time
about your single state?"

"No, she has good news. The best, in fact. She's
pregnant! The doctor says she's in good health, and the
baby will arrive in May."

Alec stood aside to let Caitlin into the elevator.
"That's terrific. Jeff must be ecstatic. He's such a great
teacher, and he loves kids. He'll make a perfect father."

"Yes, I'm thrilled to bits, except for one thing. Now
that my family can stop fretting about Merry's failure
to conceive, they've got nothing to worry about except
me. Poor old spinster Caitlin, toiling away at her job in
Washington because she can't find a man to look after
her."

He grinned. "Well, love, you have to face facts. In
less than two years you'll be turning thirty, and your
chances of snaring a man are fading fast. Heck, if I held
you up to the light, bet I'd already see the gray hair and
wrinkles."

"A few more weeks like the one I've just had and you
won't need to hold me up to the light."

They stepped into the downstairs lobby. "Bad week?" Alec inquired with genuine sympathy.

"No, a great week, but too busy." She beamed, unable to conceal her accomplishment and pride in it any longer. "I managed to find a housekeeper for the chairman of the World Bank. And he's accepted our bid on janitorial services for his entire office complex."

"Way to go, Caity!" Alec's hug was full of warmth and shared pleasure. "I know how hard you worked to get that cleaning account."

She tried to look modest and failed completely. "Sam's made me a junior partner and given me a five-thousand-dollar raise."

"Hey, this calls for a *real* celebration. Champagne, fancy French restaurant, dancing under the stars..."

She groaned. "Don't tempt me, Alec, I'm too tired. Mama Maria's is about all I can handle tonight. I need the noise and the clattering plates to keep me awake. Too much quiet French refinement and I'll nod off into my stuffed partridge."

"Okay. We'll save the French and fancy for next weekend."

Caitlin's heart gave a curious little lurch of excitement. The prospect of getting dressed up and enjoying a real night out on the town with Alec had an appeal she couldn't quite identify.

"I'd like that," she said, and then lapsed into a silence that wasn't as easy as silences between them usually were.

Alec spoke crisply. "Eight o'clock, next Saturday. It's a date. I'll pick you up at your apartment."

They stepped out onto M Street. The sidewalk was thronged with pedestrians and the road was bumper to bumper cars, trucks and delivery vans. Georgetown was patronized by yuppies, diplomats, doctors, college students and a lot of tourists, so its narrow, cobbled streets tended to be impassable at most hours of the day or night.

Caitlin assessed the bustling scene with a practiced eye. "No point in waiting for a cab," she said.

Alec agreed. "The restaurant's only ten blocks, and it's a good night for walking. Not too hot, not too cold. No humidity, no wind and a glorious sunset." He drew a satisfied breath. "I love fall."

Caitlin turned her face to catch the pleasant evening breeze. "September and October are terrific. The only problem is that five months of grungy winter come next." She zigzagged expertly between a band of street musicians and a gaggle of college students cheering a young man who had managed to balance six empty beer cans on the top of his head. She laughed, shaking off her tiredness, and seized Alec's hand.

"I'm so glad you stopped by tonight. I've missed you. What've you been doing these past couple of weeks?"

"Hiring another paralegal, trying to understand a new computer program that was supposed to cut my research time in half and is currently driving the entire office crazy. And defending Dwayne Jones on a murder charge without much success."

She looked up quickly, knowing that this was a case that had troubled him. "The verdict's in?"

"No, the trial isn't over yet, but the prosecution has the jury convinced Dwayne is guilty—I can tell by their faces."

"I haven't seen anything about Dwayne's case in the papers."

"Why would you?" Alec said with a trace of bitterness. "What's one more murder in a city that has a dozen or so each month? Drug-related shootings in the inner city happen so often they aren't news anymore. Dwayne's story isn't interesting to anyone except his mother and his sisters, and they're convinced he's going to get convicted despite the fact that he didn't kill anyone."

"Do you agree with them? Do you really believe he's innocent?"

"Nobody growing up in Anacostia is *innocent*. The kids in that project are born streetwise, or they don't survive. But Dwayne's bright and he's stayed in school, and if he can just beat this rap, he'll graduate with honors in May. Lord knows, that's a miracle all in itself. Dwayne's probably shoplifted, he may even have snatched a purse or two. But he didn't murder anyone that night, I'm sure of it. The poor kid had the bad luck to be in the wrong spot at the wrong time, and now he's facing life imprisonment for a crime he didn't commit."

"I thought you'd found witnesses to say he hadn't done the shooting."

"I had," Alec agreed grimly. "Now my witnesses have gone underground."

"Disappeared, you mean?"

"Yes, either they're afraid of offending one of the local gang leaders, or else they're simply afraid of messing with the police and the law courts. In the neighborhood Dwayne comes from, they don't view cops and lawyers and judges the way we do. I'm not a friendly civic protector—I'm the enemy. But unless I can persuade those two witnesses to trust me and resurface, Dwayne Jones doesn't have much hope."

"Do you have private detectives out looking for the witnesses?"

"You bet. Three of them, all old-timers. They're the best. If anyone can find those witnesses, they will."

Caitlin was still holding Alec's hand. She gave it a comforting squeeze, not needing to say or do anything more to let him know she understood that this sort of case ate at his professional conscience like acid. She knew that Alec had taken on Dwayne's case as a favor to the public defender's office, which meant that he would receive no pay for his work, and that the expenses connected with the case would all come straight out of Alec's pocket. If Dwayne Jones had any chance at all to get his life together, Alec Woodward was that chance. At moments like this, Caitlin felt proud to have him as a friend.

They turned onto Wisconsin Avenue. "Mama Maria's!" she exclaimed, sighting the restaurant. "Mmm, I can smell the oregano already, and the melted mozzarella."

"Keep your fingers crossed there isn't a line. I'm starving. I skipped lunch and my stomach is not happy with the situation."

They were in luck; the restaurant was crowded but not yet full. Maria Rossi, a second-generation American with the flashing black eyes of her Italian ancestors but a svelte figure straight out of *Cosmopolitan* magazine, personally directed them to a secluded table in a quiet corner of the dining room.

"You look like you need some time alone," she said, handing them the oversize menus. "Me, I always know when lovers are in turmoil. My mother was Sicilian, and she emigrated to America because the neighbors accused her of witchcraft. She had second sight, and me,

I inherited her gift. Or at least some of it. I always know when a couple's love life is in crisis. You two are deciding whether to get married, right?"

"Er... not exactly—"

"Sure you are. You want some Chianti like always, yes?" With a cheerful smile, Maria wound her way back to the reception desk, not waiting for their answers.

Caitlin chuckled. "Last time I heard that story, Maria's mother had to flee from the Nazis before they could imprison her for being such a brave resistance fighter against Mussolini's fascists."

Alec leaned back against the comfortable leather banquette. "Maybe her mother was a brave resistance fighter *and* a witch. That would be a pretty useful combination, I should think."

"Well, Maria didn't inherit her mother's gift if she thinks we're lovers, but at least she gave us the best seats in the house." Caitin crunched contentedly on a bread stick. "Gosh, it's great to relax. Remember to look like a tormented lover when Maria comes back with the wine. We don't want her to be disillusioned."

"Like this?" Alec asked.

She looked up from the menu, and for a bewildering second thought she saw such love and frustrated longing in Alec's gaze that she actually shivered. "Hey, Alec, cut it out," she said awkwardly. "You're too darn convincing."

He laughed, his eyes once again gleaming with good humor and nothing more. "Lawyers have to be three parts actor, didn't you know that?"

Maria returned with a small, straw-covered bottle of Chianti and two glasses. "Enjoy," she said, removing the cork with a single expert tug and leaving Alec to pour the wine himself.

A college student in a minuscule miniskirt brought them warm bread, bowls of green salad and wrote down their order for pizza. "It'll take twenty minutes," she explained. "The kitchen prepares each pizza to order."

"No problem. We're not in a hurry." Alec smiled and the waitress smiled back. She leaned over to top up his wineglass, making sure he received the best possible view of her generous cleavage.

Caitlin watched the waitress weave her way through the crowded tables. "You made a conquest," she said, amused. "Those hip wiggles are all for you."

"Jealous?" Alec inquired, smiling lazily.

"She's not your type."

"Isn't she? What is my type?"

Caitlin started to answer, then realized she had nothing to say. She stared at Alec in blank astonishment, holding a forgotten forkful of salad in midair.

Alec gently guided the fork back to her plate. "What is it?" he asked. "Caitlin, what did I say that was so shocking?"

She blinked, then laughed a bit stiltedly. "Your question surprised me, that's all."

"After twenty years, I'm glad I can still surprise you."

"Well, you did. The fact is I've no idea what sort of woman appeals to you. For all I know, a perky college student might be your ideal date."

"She was—fifteen years ago when I was a perky college student myself."

She smiled. "Alec you were never perky. Pseudo-sophisticated, maybe, but perky, never."

"You're nearly seven years younger than me. When I left for college you'd barely turned ten. Maybe you didn't see me as I really was."

"I *know* I didn't see you as you really were. Alec, surely you realized what a terrible crush I had on you. I thought you were God's gift to women. For years I had this recurring nightmare that you'd marry someone else before I had a chance to grow up and marry you myself."

"I seem to remember your telling me something of the sort when you were about sixteen."

Feeling a jolt of nostalgia, Caitlin took a long, slow sip of wine. "You were halfway through law school and your parents told me you were unofficially engaged. To a nurse called Jeannie Drexel, remember?"

"How could I forget? We got as far as setting the wedding date before Jeannie got smart and pointed out to me that unless we were in bed we had nothing to say to each other. I've always been grateful to her for being so perceptive."

"I was furious with you," Caitlin said. In her mind's eye, she could see the skinny, graceless young girl she'd been, red pigtails flying behind her in the wind as she cycled to the stream where Alec had gone fishing. "I told you you were making a big mistake."

"And you were quite right."

Caitlin smiled wryly. She had gained a lot of wisdom and common sense since those days, but somewhere deep in her heart she felt a little ache for all the passion and emotion she'd lost along the way. Growing up, she reflected, wasn't entirely a change for the better.

"You were very kind to me," she said. "Not many young men would have been able to let down an overwrought teenager so gently."

"You wanted me as your link to the big exciting world outside Hapsburg, Ohio, not as a husband," Alec said. "So being gentle wasn't difficult. All I had to do was remind you about going to college, and how you could have an interesting job, and your very own apartment, and the car of your choice." He grinned ruefully. "In fact, it's humiliating to look back and remember how easily I persuaded you that a career would be much more satisfying than marriage to me."

"The sixteen-year-old heart is notoriously fickle," Caitlin said. "You should never have mentioned the car. It was the prospect of owning my own BMW that did it."

The pizza arrived and the waitress took the opportunity to give Alec another wholesale review of her charms. Alec seemed too hungry to notice. He proceeded to silence his rumbling stomach with a couple of hefty slices of pizza, then poured them both a final glass of wine.

"That was delicious. The food gets better each time we come," he said. "What do you think?"

"Better and better," Caitlin agreed. "You eat the rest of the pizza, though. Otherwise I'll have to spend the entire weekend at the health club working off excess calories."

Alec helped himself to another slice. "I'm glad you were free tonight," he said after a few moments of contented munching. "I've been wanting to talk to you about something important for weeks, and I've just never managed to find the right opportunity."

"Something personal?"

"Very personal." He seemed absorbed in the task of wiping his fingers on the huge paper napkin. He looked up suddenly. "I've decided to get married."

Caitlin felt a sharp constriction in her lungs, as if someone had placed a heavy weight on her rib cage and then ordered her to carry on breathing normally. Alec was going to get married. Why was she so shocked? Perhaps because she had always assumed that Alec would remain single, like her. She swallowed hard, trying to make herself feel enthusiastic. Alec was her friend. If he had fallen in love—found a woman to marry—she ought to feel happy for him.

"Congratulations," she said, injecting as much zing into her voice as she possibly could. "I'm so pleased for you, Alec. Who is ... who is the lucky woman?"

Alec smiled cheerfully. "I've no idea. Not yet."

Caitlin stared at him blankly. "What on earth do you mean? How can you decide to get married without knowing who you want for your wife?"

"Easily," he said, "with your help. You're my best friend, you've known me for years, plus you're a woman with years of professional experience interviewing job applicants. I'm counting on you to find the right woman for me."

Caitlin was so shocked she couldn't do anything except stare at Alec in speechless amazement. She had known this man and his family for twenty years. For the past couple of years she'd have sworn she understood his thoughts and feelings almost as well as she understood her own. Listening to him, Caitlin wondered if she had ever understood him at all. The thought was so bizarre it made her feel as though the universe was tilting.

"I can't find a wife for you," she said finally. "Good grief, Alec, the very idea is absurd. We're heading into the twenty-first century, for heaven's sake. Arranged marriages have gone the way of the dinosaurs."

"Maybe it's time to reintroduce the concept," he suggested. "You know, like everyone thought plastic and polyester were the miracle products of the future.

Then we realized that maybe cotton and wood had a lot to recommend them, after all.''

She reached for her wineglass and took a hefty swallow of Chianti. Her teeth chattered against the glass, and she spared a moment to wonder why Alec's decision to look for a wife should have such a strange *physical* impact on her. She realized she felt obscurely angry, as if he had betrayed an element of their friendship by even suggesting he wanted to get married.

"I don't understand why you feel this sudden need for a wife," she said, trying to smile. "Personally I'd recommend hiring a good housekeeper. They're much easier to get rid of if they don't work out."

He leaned forward and looked at her, his eyes dark and shadowed in the flickering candlelight. "Caitlin, I'm soon going to be thirty-five. I've spent fifteen years running and pushing and striving to climb the career ladder. I don't regret those years—I'm proud of them, proud of the work I've done as a lawyer. But I've reached the stage in my life when I need something more than professional success. Getting promoted from junior partner to senior partner in my law firm isn't going to cure this ache in my gut. That's an ache caused by loneliness."

"So increase your social life," she said, refusing to acknowledge a flash of fellow feeling. "Get together with one of those nubile young law associates who are dying to date you."

"I'm tired of playing the dating game, and I'm tired of dating the people I meet professionally. The law is a fascinating occupation, but there's more to life than tort reform and indemnity clauses."

"Then take up a hobby," she snapped. "How about skiing? I remember last winter we both said we'd like to learn to ski, but we never did anything about it. Maybe this winter—"

Alec sounded impatient. "Caitlin, get real. Sports and hobbies can be a fun part of married life, but they can't be a substitute. I guess I've finally grown up. I've realized over the last couple of years that having a great collection of wine, a fabulous stereo system and a Persian rug to complement the leather couches in my living room doesn't turn my apartment into a home. And that's what I want, Caitlin—a home I can share with a congenial companion. I want a wife. A loving wife, a woman who'd like to help me build a home, and be the mother of my children—"

"You can hold it right there." Caitlin knew her smile was brittle, but she couldn't help it. Alec's words were pricking her skin like needles, and the more he said, the more painful it became. "You've just hit on the major problem with your neat little scenario. Finding the right wife isn't an easy job, you know—otherwise half the marriages in this country wouldn't end up in divorce court. Why do you think our agency does such a thriving business in placing nannies and housekeepers? Most of the time we're placing our recruits in a family split by divorce."

"True, there are a lot of failures, but we both know marriage doesn't have to end in the divorce court. Look at your family. Look at mine. Our parents have been contentedly married for years. Your sisters and mine couldn't be happier with their husbands."

"They're satisfied by their standards," Caitlin said. "But the women in both our families have sacrificed their entire lives to their marriages. Is that what you want from your wife? A woman whose interests are so narrow she's prepared to stay home all day experimenting with new recipes and taking your babies for walks in the park? For heaven's sake, Alec, what will you talk about to this wonderfully domesticated wife of yours five years down the road?''

"Everyday things," he said. "Maybe whether the baby got a new tooth, or whether we should treat ourselves to a vacation in Hawaii. Maybe we'll discuss ways she could combine her career with motherhood."

"How about ways that *you* could cut back on your career so that *you* could stay home and baby-sit while your wife worked full-time?"

"That, too," Alec said quietly. "I'd certainly be willing to consider taking time off from my career if that's what my wife needed in order to feel fulfilled and happy in our marriage."

He was really serious about getting married, Caitlin thought, feeling a stir of panic deep inside. She didn't want Alec to find this wonderful wife, she realized, because there was no way their unique friendship would survive after he was married.

She felt a sense of loss so acute it was physically painful, but she ignored the ache and forced herself to smile. The necessity for deception was painful in itself. In the past, she'd never had any reason to conceal her true feelings from Alec. Drat and damnation, she thought. Why did he have to change things when we were so happy?

She stretched her smile a notch wider and raised her wine glass in a toast. "Well, old friend, I can see you're determined to become a married man, so here's wishing you good luck in finding the perfect wife."

He raised his own glass in reply. "Thanks. How soon can you start your search? As you can imagine, now that I've finally decided to take the plunge, I'm anxious to start interviewing candidates."

"Alec, I can't find you a wife! There are a few things in this life that people have to do strictly for themselves, and finding a mate is one of them. Besides, I'm the worst person you could possibly ask. You know how I feel about marriage. I've never made any secret of the fact that I think it's a trap for women."

"But nobody's asking *you* to get married, Caity. We're talking about me. You're a professional personnel recruiter. Just because you don't personally know how to be a butler or a nanny doesn't mean you can't find excellent butlers and nannies for your clients."

"It may have escaped your notice," she said dryly, "but there's a difference between the duties performed by a butler and those that would be required of a wife. Our company has listings for literally hundreds of domestic helpers. We don't have any files headed 'Potential Wives.'"

"Improvise. I'm willing to pay all expenses and a five-thousand-dollar fee."

The waitress arrived to clear their plates and take orders for dessert. Caitlin had lost her appetite, but she ordered a cup of cappuccino for appearance sake. Alec ordered fresh fruit, then ruined the health effects by asking for ice cream on the top. His appetite, Caitlin thought resentfully, didn't appear to be suffering in the slightest from his sudden crazy desire to get shackled for life to some sweet young thing who would bake him cookies, bring him his slippers—and warm his bed. So far, their conversation had remained amazingly deco-

rous, all things considered. Alec hadn't said a word
about how he and his mythically perfect wife were going to conduct their affairs in the bedroom, but if ru-
mor could be believed, Alec was going to want someone
whose skills in bed were as superlative as her skills in the
kitchen.

"You're blushing," Alec said softly. "What are you
thinking about?"

"It's the wine," she lied. "You know I can't drink
more than a glass without getting all hot and bothered."

Alec leaned across the table and clasped her hand.
"Help me, Caitlin. I really do want to find a wife as
quickly as possible, and with the caseload I'm carrying
right now, I don't have the chance to meet many suitable women."

"If you're too busy to find a wife, I'd say you're too
busy to sustain a worthwhile marriage."

Alec turned away, his shoulders rigid with tension.
When he turned back, his expression was determined,
his voice grim. "You know, Caitlin, some of the most
important decisions we make are the hardest ones to
explain. You may not understand my reasons, but the
fact is, I've decided to get married. I'd like your help in
finding a wife, but if you don't feel up to the job, then
I guess I'll go to some other employment agency and
offer the assignment to them."

She had absolutely no idea what bug had gotten into
Alec, Caitlin thought testily, but she certainly wasn't
going to have him take his silly assignment to some
other company. "Services Unlimited is the best employment agency in town," she said. "If you're determined to go through with this crazy scheme, then I'm

sure our company will be able to find you the perfect bride.''

Alec beamed. ''I'm sure you're right,'' he said. ''In fact, I'm counting on it.''

CHAPTER TWO

DOT MARCHED into Caitlin's office and slapped a file folder on the desk. "I know this must be a joke," she said. "But it's Monday, and I'm half asleep. Would you please explain the punch line so we can both have a good laugh?"

Caitlin picked up the folder and read the label, although she knew quite well what it said. She'd written the tag herself a couple of hours earlier. "Client: Alec Woodward, Attorney-at-law. Position available: Wife, full-time, live-in."

Caitlin flipped open the file and glanced at the papers nestled inside. "Everything seems to be in order," she said, pretending not to notice that her secretary hovered on the verge of apoplexy. "Yep, it's all here—detailed job description, photo of client, profile of the ideal applicant, salary and benefits for the prospective wife, and details of our agency fee. Alec has agreed to pay us five thousand dollars by November first, provided I've presented at least four suitable candidates before then. If he actually marries one of our candidates, then we get a five-thousand-dollar bonus. All our usual expenses will be reimbursed by him of course."

Dot leaned down and peered closely at her boss. "You don't look crazy," she said. "You don't even look as if you have a fever. So that means this has to be some kind of a bad joke. In the first place, we're a personnel company, not a hearts-and-flowers dating agency. And in the second place, Alec Woodward doesn't need to hire anybody to find him a wife. He's got a body to die for, great teeth, thick hair and bedroom eyes. Plus he's intelligent, successful in his career and has enough money to keep the wolf from several doors. Heck, from what I've seen, he's even quite a nice guy—or at least no more of a rat than most of the men in this world. Now, explain to me why a guy with those qualifications would need to hire a domestic-services company to find him a wife."

"He's too busy to find one himself?" Caitlin suggested.

Dot's eyes popped in astonishment. "Too busy to find his own wife, but not too busy to take on the responsibilities of married life? That's a new one. Even my ex-husbands wouldn't have come up with an explanation that dumb."

Caitlin closed the file with a brisk snap. She'd had an entire weekend to rethink her Friday night conversation with Alec, and she could no longer understand why she'd been so reluctant to accept the assignment. A job search was a job search as far as she was concerned, and she prided herself on her outstanding professional ability to match client and applicant. Right now, she couldn't think of a single reason that finding a wife for Alec should be any more difficult than finding an English butler for the Japanese ambassador. On the whole, Alec's requirements for his future wife seemed a great deal more flexible than the ambassador's requirements for his butler. Caitlin returned the folder to her secretary with a cheerful smile.

"It's too late to back out now, Dot. I've accepted the assignment, and Sam's quite pleased I did. He says that with the fast pace of life today, maybe there's a renewed need for a topnotch matrimonial agency in a big, impersonal city like Washington. He wants us to consider this search for Alec's wife as a test case for our company, and if the search proves successful, he's going to evaluate merging with a major dating agency and upgrading their services to the same high standards we apply to all our other personnel services."

"Sounds to me like you and Sam stood out too long in the rain we had Saturday afternoon. You both lost your marbles in the storm." Dot tucked the offending folder under her arm. "This isn't gonna work out the way you planned, Caitlin, believe me. But of course I don't expect you or Sam to listen. I'm just the typist around here."

Caitlin grinned. "Right. I've noticed how shy and hesitant you are about expressing your opinions. Sam and I are both so intimidating."

Dot didn't deign to give a reply. With a withering look, she retreated to her own office. Two minutes later, she stuck her head back around the door. "Don't forget you have a three-o'clock appointment with Michelle Morreau. She's the fancy chef who would like a live-in position with one of our Washington bigwigs."

"I have her résumé here. On paper, she sounds like a great find."

"Yeah, but the way this day is going, she'll probably turn out to have warts on her nose and fungus growing on her chin."

Dot's gloomy predictions couldn't have been more wrong. In the flesh, Michelle Morreau proved every bit as marketable as her résumé suggested. A petite, vivacious woman in her late twenties, with sparkling eyes and a cap of shining, dark brown hair, she had trained in Paris and Switzerland before returning to the States a few weeks earlier. She arrived for her interview carrying a tray of homemade goodies so delicious even Dot was forced to admit that the applicant's skills as a pastry chef were beyond dispute.

Michelle explained that she wanted to buy a home in the Washington area and had decided that a live-in job would help her to save enough money to accumulate the down payment on a small town house before her thirtieth birthday.

Caitlin felt an immediate kinship with this woman, whose age and ambitions were not dissimilar to her own. "I have several excellent nonresident positions I could recommend to you," she said. "Unfortunately I have only one live-in position on the books at the moment. It's for a member of the cabinet who's looking for a cook."

Michelle perked up. "That sounds interesting."

"Unfortunately there's a catch. He has three young teenagers, and he wants the cook to supervise the children when he and his wife go out of town. I suspect that your cooking skills would be underutilized, but he's offering excellent pay, and their house in Chevy Chase is lovely. In view of the possible child-care duties, would you still be interested in going for an interview?"

"Yes, I think so," Michelle said after considering for a few seconds. "A cabinet member must throw a lot of big parties, which would give me the chance to show off my fancy cooking. And I come from a huge family, so I'm used to being around kids. Occasional baby-sitting would be no problem." She smiled and gave a very Gallic shrug. "My grandmother can't understand why I'm not surrounded by my own babies. She always thought I would marry young and have a clutch of children at my knees long before now."

Caitlin returned her smile. "Your family sounds like mine. My sisters have rounded up every bachelor within a fifty-mile radius of our hometown in an effort to provide me with a husband. I'm trotted out like a brood mare every time I go home on a visit."

"I'm sure they mean well." Michelle fell silent for a moment, and some of the sparkle in her expression died. "I was married once. It was the love match of the century as far as I was concerned, except that my husband asked for a divorce on our second wedding anniversary." She broke off abruptly. "I'm sorry. None of this has anything to do with the member of the cabinet and his need for a cook."

But it might have a lot to do with Alec's quest for a wife, Caitlin thought with sudden excitement. Here was a young attractive woman who liked children and didn't seem in the least opposed to the idea of marriage, despite the unhappy experience with her first husband. Caitlin felt the tingle of anticipation that always came when she was on the verge of tackling a challenging assignment. She leaned forward, elbows resting on her desk.

"Ms. Morreau, I hope you won't be offended by what I'm going to ask. It's a personal question, and you have absolutely no need to answer if you prefer not to. Whatever you reply will have no bearing on my recommendation to the cabinet member. Rest assured I'll be happy to arrange for that interview no matter what answer you give to my question."

Michelle looked intrigued. "This sounds interesting. Go ahead and ask."

"All right, here goes. Would you consider marrying again in the near future?"

"If I met the right man, I might," Michelle said. "But I sure don't have any prospects at the moment. If I take a job through your agency, Ms. Howard, you needn't worry that I'll quit any time soon."

"That wasn't why I asked the question." Caitlin realized she was drumming her fingers on the top of her desk in a nervous rhythm. She stopped at once, clasping her hands loosely in front of her. There was no reason for her to be jumpy, no reason at all. Finding Alec a wife was a straightforward business assignment, and that was exactly how she was going to approach it. Caitlin decided not to beat around the bush any longer. She plunged ahead, leaving no time for second thoughts.

"Ms. Morreau, I have a somewhat unusual position on our books at the moment, and I wonder if you might be interested in hearing about it."

"I certainly would. I often prefer unusual assignments."

Caitlin drew a deep breath. "A well-established professional man in this city is looking for a wife," she said. "Our company has agreed to select possible candidates for him to interview. Would you care to meet our client?"

Michelle recoiled visibly. "And apply for a job as someone's *wife?* Good heavens, no! This isn't a dating service, is it? I'd never have come here if I'd known it was a dating service."

"We're not a dating service, or at least not yet. I wish you'd reconsider your answer, Ms. Morreau. The man in question is an old friend of mine, and I've taken on the assignment partly as a favor to him, and partly as a test case for our company. We are the nation's premier domestic-placement company, and we believe there's scope for us to bring our expertise to bear in an area that hasn't received much attention from trained professionals. Sam Bergen, our president, feels that the modern world is doing such a terrible job of pairing up potential spouses that maybe the time has come to rediscover some of the older methods."

"I think the modern world has moved past the point of needing arranged marriages."

"Perhaps. Frankly, you'd be participating in an experiment if you agreed to meet with this client of ours."

Michelle shook her head. "In my wildest dreams, I can't imagine that some stranger from your files would make a suitable husband for me. Besides, how do I know that he isn't a weirdo? He's almost bound to be a creep. A man who needs an employment agency to find a wife for him doesn't sound like very promising husband material."

"I've known this man and his family since grade school, and I can assure you there are no skeletons in his closet, no hereditary health problems and no reason you wouldn't find him a very attractive date." Caitlin smiled encouragingly. "My secretary insists that he's a prime hunk, and he also happens to be a very successful criminal lawyer."

"Then what's his problem? Is he ninety years old or something?"

"Thirty-five. A veritable spring chicken. Think about it, Michelle. From your point of view, what do you have to lose? Agreeing to meet my client doesn't commit you to marriage. It doesn't even commit you to a second meeting. And you just might decide that you like each other enough to pursue the relationship."

Michelle ran her fingers through her neat cap of hair. "I can't believe I'm even listening to this. It's crazy. It's insane." She half rose from her chair, then sat down again with a tiny, self-mocking laugh. "Okay, I'll admit you've caught my attention. I *am* crazy, crazy enough to be curious, at least. Have you got a picture of this man?"

"Right here," Caitlin said, pleased at her forethought in insisting Alec provide a photo. They'd gone back to his apartment on Friday evening and spent nearly three hours composing Alec's biographical statement, striving to make it as appealing as possible to prospective wives. Then they'd outlined the practical and financial arrangements that Alec wanted to include in a legally notarized prenuptial agreement. He might be reckless enough to consider finding his wife through an employment agency, but it seemed he still retained enough lawyerly caution to want a rock-solid prenuptial contract.

Michelle took the file. As she inspected Alec's photo, Caitlin could see her expression change from skepticism to dawning wonder. Finally she looked up and met Caitlin's gaze.

"This picture's been fixed, right? I mean, the man doesn't look this fabulous in real life. Good Lord, why would he be scrounging for dates? The man is sex appeal personified. And those eyes—those eyes of his are lethal. That color comes from contact lenses for sure."

"He doesn't wear contacts." Amused at Michelle's enthusiasm, Caitlin leaned over and looked again at the familiar picture. It was a publicity shot taken when Alec was elected to the partnership at the prestigious law firm of Smythe, Howell, Bernstein and Gemelli.

Alec looked amazingly handsome, Caitlin admitted. His eyes—his much admired blue eyes—seemed to laugh up at her, teasing, friendly and yet oddly provocative, promising a woman all sorts of exciting adventures if she once surrendered to their owner's magnetic charm. Caitlin had seen the photo a dozen times. Strange she'd never noticed Alec's incredible sexiness until Dot and Michelle both pointed it out.

She tucked the picture back in the file. "This picture isn't touched up at all," she said. "Alec looks just like that." Her voice sounded oddly husky, so she cleared her throat and continued briskly. "Would you like to read his personal bio? It's on that sheet of green paper."

Michelle read no more than a couple of paragraphs before her head jerked up. "I know who this man is," she said, sounding breathless. "He's Alec Woodward, the defense attorney."

"Right." Caitlin's sense of humor had returned, and she found Michelle's awed reaction diverting. "You say that as if you recognize his name."

"*Singles* magazine voted him Washington's Most Eligible Bachelor. There was a big spread on him in last month's issue. He's the lawyer who defended Cindy Carstairs on a charge of murdering her husband on an abandoned movie set."

"And won. What can I say? Services Unlimited prides itself on listing only the best clients," Caitlin joked, although inwardly she admitted to feeling impressed. Being declared Most Eligible Bachelor in a city known for its attractive, powerful and wealthy men was no small achievement. It was typical of Alec, of course, that he had never mentioned it. Caitlin and his family had only discovered he was class valedictorian at Harvard when he stood up to make his valedictory speech.

"'Five foot eleven, 180 pounds, state of Ohio junior tennis champion,'" Michelle read aloud, her voice rapt. "That's an interesting coincidence—I was captain of my high-school tennis team." She pulled out the yellow sheet that listed Alec's requirements for marital bliss.

"He wants at least one child, possibly two if his wife is agreeable, and we can reconcile the needs of the children with the demands of our careers. He'd like to stay in Washington for the next few years, but he's willing to consider living in other major cities if his wife prefers that. He doesn't like living in the country, although eventually he'd like to buy a cottage for weekend retreats." Michelle sighed happily. "Alec, baby, you sound like my perfect man."

Springing to her feet, Michelle closed the file and returned it to Caitlin's desk. "Ms. Howard, do me a favor and arrange a meeting for me with Alec Woodward as soon as you can. I'm sure he'll turn out to have some horrible major drawback, but from his file, he seems the perfect mate. The man looks sexier than a movie star, and writes with more sensitivity than a poet. Unless the full moon turns him into a werewolf, why did the women of Washington, DC, leave him on the loose for so long?"

Caitlin laughed. "Don't worry, I personally guarantee that he has no fangs. He's single because he's been too busy to think about getting married until recently. Besides, not every woman in the world wants to get married, you know, even to a man like Alec Woodward. Maybe he had an unhappy love affair, or loves the wrong woman."

Now why in the world had she said that? Caitlin wondered. She knew quite well that Alec wasn't suffering from an unsuccessful love affair. He'd had a few serious relationships in the past ten years, but they'd all been broken off by mutual consent relatively painlessly. She knew him well enough to be certain of that—didn't she?

"I guess it's possible he's nursing a broken heart," Michelle said, although her tone suggested she couldn't imagine Alec Woodward being rejected by any sane woman. "Anyway, if he's been wounded in the battle between the sexes, so much the better. I've been a victim, too, so we can comfort each other."

Caitlin bit back the retort that Alec didn't need comforting and that—if he did—she was perfectly capable of providing all the solace he needed. She knew her reaction was irrational, but perhaps it wasn't surprising that she felt this spurt of jealousy at the prospect of Michelle or some other woman taking the number-one spot in Alec's life.

The trouble was, deep down inside, she hadn't yet accustomed herself to the idea that he wanted to marry. She'd always assumed he viewed marriage much as she did: as a trap that locked men and women together in a lifelong bond that snuffed out excitement, creativity and personal growth. Of course, even in today's supposedly liberated society, women sacrificed far more than men in most marriages. Alec's independence wasn't going to be compromised just because he took a wife. Even so, there was no denying that in her heart of hearts, Caitlin felt a knife thrust of betrayal. Alec was her best friend, darn it! She'd been counting on him to be there for her—always.

She pretended to rummage through her papers for a moment while she regained control of her emotions. It wasn't more than a few seconds before she managed to pin on a bright, professional smile.

"So, Michelle, when can I arrange a first meeting for you and my client?" *Yes, that was better. Think of him as "my client," not as "my dear friend Alec."*

Michelle smiled back, a cheerful, uncomplicated smile. "The sooner the better! As you know, I'm not working at the moment, so my hours are very flexible. Any time Mr. Woodward is available, I'm willing to meet him."

"What's your favorite restaurant?"

"Maison Blanche, you know the one? Right by the White House."

"Great choice," Caitlin commented, relieved to find her professional instincts once again completely in charge. "That's a favorite with Alec, too. I'll call him this afternoon and try to set up a lunch or dinner date within the next week. In the meantime, would you like me to contact the cabinet member and arrange an interview for the position as his cook?"

"I think you'd better do that," Michelle said, her voice wry. "I need to line up something a bit more mundane than a date with Alec Woodward if I'm going to keep my head out of the clouds."

Escorting Michelle out to the reception area and the bank of elevators, Caitlin dismissed her earlier moment of doubt. "I'll be in touch some time this week," she promised, thinking that the wife-search was really going far better than she'd expected.

"I'll be waiting." Michelle blushed at her own eagerness, then smiled with just a hint of sauciness.

"Goodbye, Ms. Howard. This has surely been an interesting afternoon!"

Alec would really enjoy Michelle's company, Caitlin decided, returning swiftly to her office. What's more, she was just the sort of cute, cheerful young woman that Alec's mother would like to have as a daughter-in-law. Yes, all in all, this had been a very successful interview. Caitlin had every reason to be pleased with her first candidate for the role of Mrs. Alec Woodward.

"Did I hear right?" Dot demanded. "Are you recommending that woman as a prospective wife for Alec Woodward?"

"Yes. Any objections?"

"None you'd be willing to listen to."

Caitlin grinned. "You're just a man-hater. She's sweet and I'm sure Alec will love her."

"For a smart woman, boss, you are sometimes amazingly dumb." Dot sighed gustily. "But then, I guess I can't talk. Smart women are always dumb where men are concerned. We're made that way so men don't have to walk around feeling permanently inferior."

Caitlin sat down at her desk, ignoring Dot's disapproving glower. In a world where time was replacing money as the commodity in shortest supply, why shouldn't busy, successful people hire professionals to find ideal spouses for them? If she could provide Alec with a suitable wife, Sam Bergen would appoint her vice president in charge of the new "matrimonial services" division. And if she made a success of that new division, maybe her dream of a full partnership would come true years earlier than she'd hoped.

Caitlin smiled ruefully, well aware that she was building tall castles on shallow foundations. Before she could dream of partnerships, she'd first have to get Alec successfully married off. She reached for the phone and dialed his office.

His secretary answered with the expected news that he was still in court. "He'll stop by to collect his messages as soon as he leaves the courtroom," she added.

"Tell him I'd like to come around and see him tonight, Betty, maybe after dinner, if that's okay. I have some exciting news for him."

Betty was middle-aged, super-efficient and devoted to Alec's well-being. For reasons Caitlin had never been able to fathom, Betty seemed to dislike her intensely. On this occasion, as always, she sounded as if talking to Caitlin was slightly less pleasurable than sucking on a lemon.

"Thank you for calling, Ms. Howard. I'll see that Mr. Woodward gets your message. However, he's very tired, and this Dwayne Jones case is causing him a lot of extra work."

"I won't keep him up late," Caitlin promised, wondering how Betty managed to make her feel so guilty when, in reality, she had nothing to reproach herself for. "The news I have is going to please Alec a lot, I promise."

"I'll pass on your message," Betty said dourly, and Caitlin could almost see the disapproving flare of the secretary's nostrils. *Oh well,* she thought, hanging up the phone. *I guess I can't expect everyone in the world to like me.* But tonight when she saw Alec, she'd ask him just what she had done to offend the woman.

CHAPTER THREE

CAITLIN COULD SMELL the coffee brewing as soon as Alec opened the door to his penthouse apartment. "Mmm, you're a wonderful man," she said, brushing her cheek against his in an absentminded greeting. "How did you know I skipped coffee and dessert?"

He grinned. "Because you always skip coffee and dessert whenever you come to visit me."

She yawned and stretched luxuriously on his expensive leather sofa, adjusting the throw pillows behind her back for maximum comfort. "You shouldn't keep imported Belgian chocolates in your fridge, and then I wouldn't be such a miserable scrounger."

"But how could I be sure you'd keep coming to visit me without my fancy chocolates?"

She laughed. "Darn, my secret's out! I love you only for your Belgian truffles."

Alec feigned heartbreak as he disappeared into his small but state-of-the-art kitchen. "Betty says you have important news for me," he called out over the rattle of coffee cups.

"The best. I've found you a wife. Or I should say a potential wife." She chuckled. "I'm not insisting that you propose to my first candidate, although she is terrific."

The cups stopped rattling. Silence descended for a second or two, and then Alec reappeared in the doorway, holding two mugs of coffee in one hand and a gold-foil box of chocolates in the other. He set both coffee and chocolates on the low table in front of the sofa before sitting down next to Caitlin.

"You don't look very pleased by my news," she said. "I thought you'd be amazed and impressed by my efficiency. Not even twenty-four hours on the job, and already I've lined up a prime candidate."

"I *am* impressed. I'm overwhelmed." Alec appeared afflicted by sudden restlessness. He got up from the sofa and walked over to the stereo, flipping through his collection of CDs with none of his usual dexterity. "I guess I'd expected to discuss my basic requirements some more before you went ahead and set up the first interview."

"Alec, we spent most of Friday night discussing your ideal wife. I feel I have a really good handle on what you're looking for. Trust me, Michelle is going to be perfect. I brought you a copy of her résumé." Caitlin handed it over, then turned her attention to choosing a chocolate. "Michelle's a cordon bleu chef," she pointed out. "Trained in Paris. Twenty-nine years old, loves children, likes to play tennis, and she's really cute."

Alec looked up from the résumé. "Blond? Brunette?"

"Dark brunette, with a pixie smile that'll melt your heart."

"She certainly sounds intriguing. When can I meet her?"

"As soon as you have some spare time. She'd like to join you for a meal at the Maison Blanche restaurant."

"The one right by the White House?"

"Yes. Naturally, she wants the first meeting to be somewhere public."

"Of course, I never expected anything else. Maybe you could set up a dinner for Friday night? I should be free by then. The Dwayne Jones trial goes to the jury tomorrow, and I don't imagine it will take them more than a few hours to reach a verdict."

Caitlin looked up anxiously. "Did you find your witnesses?"

"One of them. He's an ex-druggie in a rehab program, so the jury may or may not believe him, but at least he took the stand and swore that he and Dwayne were in a café eating dinner, not in the liquor store where the shooting took place. The DA kept hammering him, but he told the same story as Dwayne—they only ran away because they didn't want to be caught up in the fighting, not because they'd fired the shots."

"That should be enough for reasonable doubt, shouldn't it?"

"I hope so." Alec finally found a CD to please him. He put the disc into the player, and the strains of a Debussy prelude drifted with soft, full-toned clarity into the living room. Caitlin listened in unaccustomed silence until the final chord had died away, her former exuberance pierced by a shaft of melancholy.

Alec hadn't rejoined her on the sofa. He sat in a chair to one side of the empty fireplace, his expression remote, almost austere, as he sipped his coffee. "What's bothering you, Caity?" he asked quietly.

Embarrassed by her thoughts, she felt herself blush, but she answered truthfully, because honesty was at the core of her relationship with Alec. "This sounds selfish," she admitted, "but I was feeling jealous of your future wife. I enjoy your company so much, Alec. There'll be a real gap in my life once you're married."

If she had expected him to reassure her, to tell her that nothing would change, she was disappointed. "Yes," he agreed. "Things will be quite different when I'm married." Politely he added, "But of course we can still be friends."

"Not friends like we are now," Caitlin said. "Your wife wouldn't be too pleased if she had to put up with my dropping in for coffee and sympathy whenever I'd had a rough day at the office."

"I guess that would be a bit much," Alec agreed. "I'll miss all the wonderful times we've had, Caity, but I've reached the stage in my life where I realize that having a successful career and a wide circle of acquaintances will never be enough to stop me from feeling lonely. I'm finally ready to make a full-scale commitment to a woman, despite what I'll have to give up." He smiled wryly. "Of course, I feel like I'm about to jump off a high cliff without a parachute, but I'm willing to make the leap. I'm tired of hot dates that lead nowhere. I'm tired of tiptoeing around my deepest emotions for fear of blundering into someone else's space. I need a woman who's willing to relate to me with total honesty. I'm tired of secrets, Caity. After a while, they poison any relationship."

He couldn't possibly realize how much his words hurt. Caitlin's body jerked ramrod straight in protest. "But you and I already have that sort of intimacy, Alec! Good grief, we tell each other *everything*. I can't imagine a more honest relationship than ours!"

"You're deceiving yourself," he said, his voice laced with weariness. "For people who've known each other as long as we have, Caity, the amazing thing is how much we *don't* reveal, how many secrets we struggle to keep hidden from each other."

If Alec had grabbed a stick and physically beaten her, Caitlin couldn't have felt more shocked. "Maybe you feel that way," she said, her voice shaking. "But I have absolutely no secrets from you, Alec. Not one."

"You can't mean that. I can think of dozens. Most of them important."

"Name one!"

He looked at her consideringly for a long, tense moment. "All right," he said at last. "Are you a virgin, Caitlin?"

Her mouth opened, but no words came. After several edgy seconds she found her voice again. "That's not a secret, it's just irrelevant. My sex life is something intensely personal, something that there's no reason for the two of us to discuss."

"But it's rather a fundamental thing for a man not to know about a woman he sees so often, wouldn't you agree?"

She shook her head. "Our relationship is based on longterm friendship not...not physical attraction. We're friends, not potential lovers."

"Even friends talk about sex occasionally, Caity, but we never do. It's a taboo subject between us. Why?"

She stirred restlessly against the cushions. "Maybe because everyone else talks about it all the time and, frankly, I think the whole subject is somewhat boring."

"Sex is overrated—is that what you're saying?"

"Some people seem to think it's important," she said carefully.

"But not you?"

She shrugged. "Surveys show that, by the time they've been married for two years, couples rarely make love more than three times a week. But each week they spend, on average, a hundred hours together. Let's say the lovemaking takes up three hours of their time. That leaves ninety-seven hours each week when they need to find something else they have in common. With statistics like that, how important can sex be?''

"Statistics show that one-third of the children in southeast DC suffered from malnutrition last year. That's an alarming fact, but does it help you to understand how a mother feels when it's dinnertime and she has no food to offer her kids? Statistics aren't weighted for emotional content, Caity, which is just one of the reasons they so often lie. Your statistics don't show the relative importance of those three hours of lovemaking in comparison to the ninety-seven hours spent sleeping or doing the laundry.''

"I don't need statistics to know the importance of sex is overrated. I'll bet the couple who shares a passionate interest in baseball stays married longer than the couple who shares a passionate interest in sex!''

"How about sharing a passionate interest in baseball *and* sex?'' Alec suggested mildly.

Caitlin was too full of nervous tension to sit still any longer. She jumped up and began pacing the room. "I'm beginning to think you're right about one thing—I don't understand you, Alec. These past few days, you've sprung a lot of surprises on me.''

"In that case, we're equal,'' Alec said. "You finally realize you don't understand me, and I admit I haven't understood you since the day you got engaged to David Wallace. That was four years ago last May, in case you've forgotten.''

Caitlin's heart began to pound with unreasonable speed. She paused by a pot of chrysanthemums in full bloom and tugged at a withered leaf. "I never made any secret of the fact that my engagement to David Wallace was a terrible mistake.''

"Why was it a mistake? He seemed like a nice guy.''

"I got engaged to David to please my family, not because I'd fallen in love with him. My sisters wanted him for a brother-in-law, and my parents thought he'd make the perfect son. The only problem was, I didn't really want him for a husband. Even so, I agreed to marry him, and when I broke off the engagement, I hurt him quite a lot, and I feel very guilty about the way I behaved." She swung around accusingly. "You know all this, Alec. You were the man who lent me his shoulder to cry on when I was trying to break off the engagement, remember?"

"Vividly," he said. "And I've been waiting for the past three years for you to admit the truth of why you really ended your engagement to David.''

Caitlin stopped shredding the chrysanthemum leaf and stared at Alec in bewilderment. She rubbed her forehead, trying to ease the start of a nagging headache. "I'm sorry," she said. "I've no idea what you're talking about.''

"On the day David got married to Kirstin Steinbeck you left their wedding reception and came to see me. You spent the entire night in my apartment. We sat up in this very room and talked for ten hours straight. And you know the most amazing thing of all? Somehow we managed to spend all that time together without once mentioning your engagement to David. So let's not kid ourselves about how honest and open and confiding our relationship is.''

"You never asked me about my feelings for him! You've never mentioned his name from that day to this!''

Alec smiled tiredly. "The night of David's wedding, you wanted comfort from me, Caity. Comfort and companionship, not soul-searching inquiry and reckless honesty. And you still want the same things. I know the rules of our relationship. I knew I wasn't allowed to ask about David. We're not allowed to probe each other's deepest emotions. That's how we keep our friendship in balance."

"How can you say that? We don't have rules," she declared vehemently. "For heaven's sake, Alec, you're picking on isolated incidents and inflating them out of all proportion."

"If you really believe that, then I guess we have different opinions about what's important. It's eighteen months since David married. Eighteen months, according to you, during which we've been best friends without a single secret between us. And yet I still don't know why you were so upset by his marriage. *You* broke off the engagement, after all. *He* didn't dump you. Did you expect him to remain single and grieving forever?"

"Of course not." Caitlin felt stifled, as if the intensity of her feelings had somehow drained all the oxygen from Alec's apartment. She walked over to the window, keeping her back turned toward him. After a long silence, she heard herself say, "I've never told anyone this. In fact, I've scarcely even admitted the truth to myself. It wasn't the reality of *David* getting married that upset me—it was something more subtle. Seeing him and Kirstin together and so much in love forced me to accept that I was never going to get married myself. And that realization hurt a lot more than I'd expected. I've always claimed that I want a career and an independent life-style, but deep inside me, I guess I had this secret belief that there was a man somewhere out there in the big world who was going to sweep me off my feet and make domesticity seem like heaven.''

"And David wasn't the man."

"Much more than that. Watching David get married, I realized that for me there wasn't *ever* going to be a Mr. Right.''

Alec had crossed the room to stand behind her. Gently he put his hands on her shoulders and turned her around, tilting her chin up so that she was forced to look at him. His eyes were dark and intent but, she was relieved to see, contained no trace of pity. "Why not?''

"Because I'm not capable of falling in love,'' she admitted, trying her best not to sound self-pitying and knowing she failed. "David was just the last in a long string of men I liked, but never managed to love. He was the nicest, kindest person you could ever hope to meet. I wanted to love him, and I simply couldn't. The earth didn't move when he looked at me. Heck, half the time I didn't notice whether he was looking at me or not. When he kissed me...'' She broke off, not sure whether to laugh or cry.

"When he kissed you...'' Alec prompted.

Caitlin confessed the humiliating truth. "I realized after we'd been engaged for a couple of months that I used the time when David kissed me to plan my work schedule for the next day. I'd close my eyes and visualize the agenda for my upcoming meetings while David was pouring his heart and soul into a caress. As soon as I realized what was happening, I knew our engagement had to end.''

Alec laughed, and she shook her head ruefully. "Honestly, Alec, it's not funny. I've thought about this for a long time, and I've decided I must have some sort of defective gene or a missing hormone or something. I'm envious when I see other couples genuinely in love, but I can't begin to imagine what they feel."

"For a woman with defective genes, Caity, you'll be delighted to hear that you look entirely normal. In fact, you look great."

"Thanks for the vote of confidence. But the truth is, Alec, I'm twenty-eight years old, and I've never come close to feeling all those crazy things everyone else seems to feel a dozen times before their twentieth birthday. By the time they were in the fifth grade, my sisters were already romantic veterans. Contrast them with me. I was so clueless I never understood I was supposed to fall madly in love with Tommy Winkler because he kept pulling my pigtails!"

"Caity, love, you aren't defective—you were clearly surrounded by clods. Now, a suave Cassanova like me never went in for crude tactics like pulling pigtails. Lord no! I found that tripping girls in the playground worked *much* better."

Caitlin laughed. "If you'd tried tripping me up, I'd have bopped you over the head with my schoolbag. Which probably proves I've been a lost cause since third grade."

"Mmm. Or it might prove you had amazingly well developed common sense."

She sighed. "Common sense isn't necessarily a blessing, Alec. From what I've seen, common sense is the last thing you need if you're planning to fall in love."

"You fell in love at least once," Alec reminded her. "Remember our dramatic confrontation on the banks of the trout pond when you declared passionate and undying devotion to me?"

"My one and only experience of a genuine teenage crush," Caitlin agreed. "But you're forgetting something important."

"What's that?"

"It took you less than half an hour to talk me out of my supposedly lifelong devotion. When Megan was sixteen, she cried herself to sleep for a whole month because Greg Bardok decided to take someone else to the senior prom. And she didn't even like Greg all that much!"

"Your sisters are lucky people. They realized early on what they wanted out of life to make them happy. Some of us take a lot longer to learn who we are and what we're going to do with our lives."

"True. And I guess I learned at David's wedding that I was never going to fall in love deeply enough to make a good marriage."

"Come on, Caity, you're too young to be making such sweeping statements."

She shook her head. "Falling in love isn't anywhere close on my horizon."

"Don't tempt fate. The poets all seem to agree that's one of the strange things about love—it so often takes you by surprise, creeping up when you least expect it. And then, wham! Before you know what's hit you, you're suffering an acute attack of love sickness."

Her laugh held just a touch of wistfulness. "I don't know how I did it, Alec, but somehow, somewhere, I got immunized against that particular disease."

He looked down at her, his gaze sober. "Okay, maybe you're never going to fall wildly, insanely, passionately in love with someone, but that doesn't mean you can never find a man who would make you an acceptable husband and a good father for your children."

She could feel herself blush fire-engine red. "All right, I admit it. I'm a romantic at heart and I can't imagine promising to share my life with a man unless I've fallen head over heels in love with him. Women make so many sacrifices when they marry that it seems to me you need to be fathoms deep in love before the arrangement is worth it."

"Then you must disapprove of my decision to find a wife through your agency. Realistically, we both know I'm not likely to fall in love with any of your candidates."

"Marriage means different things to different people," she said. "You're a man. Perhaps falling in love isn't so important to you. After all, your life is likely to change far less than your wife's."

His gaze darkened. "Love is very important to me," he said softly. "But I guess to a certain extent I'm like you. I've just about given up on the impossible dream."

She'd been so intent on their conversation she hadn't noticed how close they'd moved to each other. To her surprise, Caitlin realized their bodies were almost touching. Alec's arms were clasped lightly around her waist and the pressure of his hands at the small of her back suddenly made her feel hot and restless deep inside. From a long way away, she heard herself ask, "Have *you* ever been in love, Alec?"

"A long time ago."

He didn't say anything more, and she prompted him. "With that nurse, Jeannie Drexel?"

"No. Like I told you, Jeannie and I shared nothing more than an acute attack of lust." Alec stared into the distance, obviously conjuring up memories that still had the power to hurt. "There was someone else.... It must be more than four years ago that I fell in love with her."

"Things didn't work out for you?"

"No."

The monosyllable sounded unbearably bleak, and Caitlin's throat had become so dry it hurt to draw breath. She swallowed hard. "I think, maybe, right around that time... your mother hinted to me that you were hoping to get married. But she never mentioned anyone's name.... And then I got engaged to David, and I didn't see much of you for a while...."

"My family never really knew the whole story, just that I was deeply in love and the woman had decided to marry another man."

"Alec, I'm so sorry. You sound as if it still hurts."

He looked down at her, visibly dragging himself back into the present. "Yeah, well, I've learned to live with the situation, I guess. Sometimes we can't have the one thing we want most."

Caitlin was so accustomed to thinking of Alec as striding through life, successful, confident and un-scathed by trauma, that it was hard for her to readjust her mental images. Looking up at him, and seeing the shadows that still lingered in his eyes at the memory of his unsuccessful love affair, she felt an unexpected rush of protective sympathy. She reached up and stroked his cheek in a hesitant gesture of consolation. To her sur-prise, Alec caught her hand and held it tight within his own. Then, even more astonishing, he turned her hand over and dropped a kiss in the center of her palm.

"Trust me, Caity, twenty-eight isn't too late to fall in love," he said softly. "Maybe you should let a few of your barricades down and see what happens."

She and Alec were still standing uncomfortably close. Her skin prickled where Alec's fingers held her, and deep in the pit of her stomach she felt the flicker of a hot, hungry flame. The sensations were odd, unfamiliar—and she didn't like them one bit. She leaned against the window frame, creating an inch or two of welcome space between herself and Alec.

He was usually sensitive to her moods, but tonight he didn't seem to notice her warning signals. Instead of dropping his hold and moving away, he leaned forward, his head bending slowly toward hers.

"Sometimes common sense can be taken too far," he murmured.

"Wh-what do you mean?"

His lips hovered no more than a hairbreadth from hers. "I mean this," he said, and brought his mouth down on hers, hard and commanding.

Caitlin closed her eyes. She wasn't planning her work schedule; she wasn't thinking about anything. Except, maybe, that Alec didn't kiss in the least like David. Or the congressman from Kentucky. Or the curator from the Smithsonian.

Alec tightened his hold around her waist. The flame deep inside her flickered once more, then roared out of control.

Caitlin surrendered herself to the conflagration.

CHAPTER FOUR

DOT GLANCED at her watch. "It's nearly five-thirty," she said. "And it's Friday the thirteenth. What's happened to Sam? How come he's missing such a golden opportunity for predicting disaster?"

"He's already left the office," Caitlin said. "He went to meet his daughter at the airport. Remember, she's arriving home from Europe today."

"No wonder the place is so peaceful. Well, if Sam's already left, I'd better go home right away, before you decide to throw a tantrum in his place."

Caitlin winced. "Have I been that bad to work with this week?"

"Oh, not too terrible, all things considered. Probably no worse than a lion with raging toothache."

"Good Lord, Dot, didn't they teach you anything in secretarial college? You aren't supposed to be honest with your boss—you're supposed to soothe my irritated nerves. I need sympathy—this has been a tough week."

"True, and from what I've seen, Michelle Morreau's frequent phone calls have been right at the top of your problem list. If you don't want her to marry your hunky lawyer friend, how come you fixed up their date tonight?"

Caitlin blinked. "Michelle's dinner date with Alec isn't causing my bad mood, of course it isn't. Why should it?"

"You tell me."

"Good grief, I'm thrilled about their meeting! It's a positive first step in an interesting business project—"

The door to the office flew open with a crash and Sam, white hair spiking into a halo around his bald pate, burst into the room. "My car has a flat tire and I can't get a cab to take me to the airport! Jodie's going to arrive and I'm going to miss her!"

Caitlin checked her watch. Five-thirty on the button. She and Dot exchanged half-amused glances. "Don't worry, Sam, I'm sure Jodie's much too sensible to do anything foolish." Caitlin spoke soothingly as she reached for the phone. "What airline is she flying with? We'll leave a message to say you're on your way and that she should wait in the baggage-claim area. Then I'll call for a limo. You've used Bob Cox's service before, and you're a good customer. I'm sure he can get someone around here within twenty minutes, even on a Friday evening."

Sam's shoulders hunched forward in dejection. "The airlines never pass on messages," he said gloomily. "Jodie will have left before I get anywhere near Dulles airport. You know what traffic's like at this time on a Friday."

His air of subdued defeat was so unusual that Caitlin felt a spurt of concern. She walked around to the front of her desk and looked down at her diminutive boss. "Sam, what's really the problem here? Your daughter is a competent grown woman, who just graduated from college with high honors. She isn't about to vanish in a puff of smoke if you're a couple of minutes late to meet her plane."

"Jodie isn't a grown woman, she's a girl!" Sam roared with some of his old fire. "What's more, she's a girl without a grain of sense in her head."

"Uh-oh," Dot said. "Now I get it. You've been up to your old tricks, Sam, don't try to deny it. You've been fighting with Jodie, haven't you? Good Lord, you shouldn't be allowed anywhere near a long-distance phone when your children are out of town."

Sam's round pink cheeks flushed bright red. "Jodie and I had a bit of an argument," he admitted.

"How big is a bit?" Dot demanded sternly.

Sam scowled. "I guess if I don't arrive at the airport right on time, Jodie will think I'm not coming to meet her. And I don't know where she'll go next." He crossed his arms, managing to look pleading and defiant all at once. "Jodie hung up on me when I tried to talk some sense into her last week. I don't know what's getting into kids these days. She's twenty-two years old, wears three earrings in one ear, and thinks she knows more than a man who's fifty-eight—"

"Tell me the sob story while we're driving," Dot interjected briskly. "I'll give you a ride out there."

"You will?" Sam's chubby face creased into a smile of pathetic gratitude. "Thanks, Dot. Thanks a million. I'll never forget this. I really owe you one."

"Just remember that when you're handing out the Christmas bonuses," Dot said dourly. "And next time your daughter goes overseas, don't call her unless you can manage to be pleasant."

"She's not going abroad again!" Sam yelled. "If she thinks I'm going to have her studying tsetse flies in Africa or any other damn fool thing, then she's mistaken.

Environmental biologist, indeed! Why can't she be a teacher like her sister, or stay at home like her mother did? She doesn't need the money. She should concentrate on meeting a nice young man so she can get married and settle down in Washington, near her family."

"So you can yell at her in person, instead of just over the phone?" Dot asked sweetly. "Come on, Sam, quit talking and let's get rolling. And you'd better promise me right now that you're not going to start arguing with Jodie as soon as you meet her, or else I'll withdraw my offer of a ride to the airport. People who get into my car are expected to behave themselves."

Caitlin watched in astonishment as Sam meekly promised to be the soul of discretion and trotted behind Dot out of the office. At moments like these, she wondered if she understood even the most superficial details about the male sex. Who would have thought Dot could control Sam's volatile temper with such apparent ease? Although, come to think of it, Dot was usually the person who calmed his Friday-night jitters.

With Sam's explosion taken care of, there was nothing to stop Caitlin from catching up on the week's paperwork. She returned to her chair and shuffled listlessly through the stack of files needing her attention. Before very long, she was stifling yawns and staring at the dial of her watch. Five-fifty. Time seemed to be moving incredibly slowly. In about two hours from now, Alec would be meeting Michelle Morreau for the first time. She wondered what Michelle would wear. Nothing too elaborate if she was smart enough to follow Caitlin's advice. Alec disliked frilly, fussy clothes on a woman. Perhaps she should give Michelle a call and remind her to choose something casually elegant and understated.

Caitlin reached for her Rolodex in search of Michelle's number, then let her hand fall back onto the desk. She shouldn't repeat her advice, shouldn't work too hard to make this evening a success. When Alec and Michelle met, they would either hit it off or they wouldn't, and Caitlin would be doing neither of them a favor if she tried to push them into a long-term relationship that wasn't exactly right for both of them.

She forced herself to read a few more files, realized she hadn't understood a word in any of them and finally admitted defeat. Her mind wasn't on work. She didn't want to think about finding a nanny for the assistant editor at the *Washington Post*. She didn't want to think about candidates for a housekeeping position at the White House. For some reason, she especially didn't want to think about perky, attractive Michelle Morreau. All she wanted to think about was last Monday night and how it had felt when Alec kissed her.

Terrifying was the word that sprang into Caitlin's mind. When Alec kissed her, she had felt as if she were tumbling downward on the fastest, most frightening stretch of a giant roller coaster. But terror wasn't the only emotion she'd experienced. For a few amazing, wonderful seconds her body had sprung into vibrant life, quivering with the shock of a dozen new and intriguing sensations. It had seemed as if, in Alec's arms, the whole world took on new meaning, and she trembled on the very edge of self-discovery. Then exhilaration turned to panic, and she pushed him away, clamping her lips together in a hard, straight line to stop them from trembling.

Alec hadn't attempted to take her back into his arms or to renew their kiss. Instead, he stood quite still, not touching her, just looking. Just looking—with those bright blue eyes that everyone suddenly seemed determined to point out were lethally sexy. He looked at her, damn him, and didn't say a single word.

"Why did you do that?" she'd demanded finally just to break the silence. Her voice sounded high and squeaky rather than cool and sophisticated, but that couldn't be helped. At least she'd resisted the urge to do something adolescent and melodramatic like slapping his face.

He didn't smile or apologize and his gaze never wavered. "It seemed like something we both wanted—something we've both wanted for a long time."

"Not me," she responded instantly and with absolute conviction. "Alec, we're *friends* and that wasn't a friendly kiss."

"No," he agreed. "It sure wasn't."

He still hadn't sounded as if he was apologizing, and Caitlin hadn't been willing to pursue the conversation any further. She turned her back on him, wrapping her arms tightly around her waist, as if a firm grip on her body could get all her rampaging feelings under control again. She hated the way she was feeling, and she was angry with the man whose kiss had made her feel that way. She breathed deeply, searching for calm.

"I should leave," she'd said, staring blindly at her watch. "It's late."

"But maybe not too late."

"It's nearly midnight."

"Yes," he'd agreed. "So it is."

Superficially their conversation had made little sense, and yet once again she'd chosen not to probe beneath the surface of his words. The past few days had produced too many shocks as far as her relationship with Alec was concerned, and she hadn't had the mental fortitude to deal with any more surprises that night. Her life was going just the way she wanted it to go, with short- and long-term goals neatly in place. Her course had been mapped out ever since she'd graduated from high school, with every stage of her career carefully charted—in a straight line up. A kiss, however odd it made her feel, couldn't be permitted to make an impact on such well-laid plans.

Determined to conquer her strange skittishness, Caitlin had swung around and glared at Alec. "Thanks for the coffee and chocolates," she muttered. "Like I said, it's getting late. I'd better leave."

"Right. Well, come back any time. I enjoy your company." He'd suddenly seemed amused, and that infuriated her. He kept up an easy flow of polite conversation while she stuffed her arms into the sleeves of her jacket and collected her purse. She answered him in gruff monosyllables, longing to escape.

Caitlin had left Alec's apartment still seething. By the time she'd arrived home, she realized her anger was out of all proportion to the events that had taken place. In today's freewheeling society, a kiss—any kiss—ranked about a minus-three on the Richter scale of emotional significance. But that insight didn't seem to change her feelings about the incident. What was even odder, her anger hadn't faded over the past five days. It still lodged, like an ill-digested meal, somewhere in the pit of her stomach. Right now, remembering Alec's kiss, she could feel a familiar arrow of emotion pierce her, and she didn't like the hot, sharp feeling one little bit.

Abandoning the pretense of resuming her work, she locked her papers into a file cabinet before shrugging into her suit jacket and picking up her briefcase. She would stop off at the health club and join one of the aerobics classes. Perhaps vigorous exercise would ease her attack of Friday-night blues. What was happening to her well-ordered life? She was never at loose ends or stressed out by overwork, and yet this was the second Friday in a row she'd felt on edge and . . . lonely.

The elevator doors slid open just as she walked out into the lobby. Alec, looking tired but cheerful, waved in greeting. "Hi, Caity! You're the very person I came searching for."

"Well, here I am." She didn't say anything more because her breath was suddenly coming in quick, jumpy little gasps and she didn't want him to notice her strange reaction.

Of course he noticed at once. "Your voice is husky," he said. "Are you catching a cold?"

"No, not at all. I'm fine."

"Good." He took her arm and followed her into the elevator. With tremendous difficulty, she refrained from jerking away. The doors glided shut and her heart started to thump hard against her ribs. He was standing so close she could smell the cologne he wore, something exotic she didn't recognize. For a moment she had the craziest urge to bury her face in the crook of his neck and breathe deeply. Fortunately, common sense reasserted itself before she gave in to the ridiculous impulse.

Nevertheless, she felt clammy with relief when the doors opened and they emerged onto the sidewalk. Alec moved away from her as he pushed back his shirt cuff to look at his watch. "You're leaving work early tonight, aren't you?" he said. "It's barely six o'clock."

"I have a date," she replied, which wasn't exactly a lie. She supposed the seven-o'clock aerobics class could be termed a date.

"Going somewhere exciting?"

Last week she would have told him the truth without hesitation. But ever since their dinner at Mama Maria's, Caitlin knew their old intimacy had vanished, disappearing into this uncomfortable tension she had no idea how to handle. So she smiled brightly and evaded a direct answer. "Oh, just the usual Friday-night sort of stuff. How about you, Alec? Did you get a verdict in the Dwayne Jones case?"

"We sure did! The jury found Dwayne not guilty. Isn't that terrific?"

"It's wonderful," she said. "Congratulations on a major victory, Alec."

He beamed, the picture of a relaxed man, balanced on the crest of success. "This has been a pretty good week, all in all. Justice is served in the Dwayne Jones case, and tonight I get to meet the woman who may agree to become my wife. I guess this is a night for celebration."

"I'm delighted you're so happy with life." Caitlin felt ashamed of the acid she heard in her voice. She forced herself to meet Alec's gaze, then wished she hadn't when her stomach looped into a tight knot. "Are you all set for the big meeting with Michelle?" she managed to ask.

He grinned. "Shaved, showered and groomed for success. Didn't you smell my new cologne? The saleswoman assured me it's guaranteed to send women insane with desire for my manly body." He leaned closer. "Is she right?"

Caitlin swallowed hard. "Not in my case, but I'm not the woman you're hoping to attract."

"True, but she promised a one-hundred-percent success rate." He smiled. "Maybe I should demand my money back."

He sounded so cheerful Caitlin's black mood darkened even further. She felt a sudden burst of resentment at his insensitivity. The world's most thick-skinned clod should have been able to see the sparks of tension flying off her body, and Alec had never been either thick-skinned or insensitive, at least until last week. In fact, his instant awareness of her moods had always been something she'd particularly valued.

Tonight, however, Alec seemed impervious to her signals. He put his arm companionably around her waist as they crossed the street and didn't notice when she stiffened. "Let's grab a drink at Hogan's bar," he said. "I want to show you the gift I've bought for Michelle. You can tell me if you think it's suitable."

"I don't really have much time. . . ."

"No? Oh, well, we can skip the drink. Just take a quick peek at my gift and tell me what you think." Alec stopped outside the bar and delved into a foil bag from the city's most expensive jewelry store. He extracted a deep blue gift box and pulled off the lid with a flourish. "What do you think?"

Nestled in a bed of pale blue satin was an exquisite miniature of a crystal princess kissing an ugly, but ecstatic-looking crystal toad.

"Do you like it?" Alec asked, sounding anxious. "Do you think it'll appeal to Michelle?"

"It's lovely," Caitlin admitted. "And I'm sure Michelle will like it a lot."

"That's a relief," Alec said. "First impressions are so important, don't you agree? Once a woman has a certain idea of a man fixed in her head, I've found it's virtually impossible to change it. Take you and me, for example. We've considered ourselves next-door neighbors and childhood friends for so long, I can't imagine what it would take to change our relationship, can you?''

A week ago Caitlin would have protested that nothing could change their relationship, ever. Now she knew better. "Our relationship has already changed," she said. "In fact, I realize now it changed as soon as you told me you were planning to get married."

Alec looked at her. For the first time that evening, he wasn't smiling. "I didn't think you'd be honest enough to admit that," he said quietly. With an abrupt movement, he shut the lid of the jewelry box and put it back into the bag. "Remember our date tomorrow night, Caity, to celebrate your promotion. Eight o'clock at your apartment. I'll pick you up."

"You're having a busy weekend, aren't you? Twirling around the dance floor tonight with Michelle Morreau and with me tomorrow."

"Do you twirl on the dance floor?" Alec asked. "You know, we've never danced together, not even at your sisters' weddings. I wonder how that happened?"

"Coincidence," Caitlin said with a shrug. "It must have been sheer coincidence."

"Yes, I'm sure it was." Alec squinted into the gathering gloom and spotted a taxi at the nearby intersection. He stepped out to the curb, waved his arm, and twenty seconds later the empty cab screeched to a halt beside him. Laughing, he turned to Caitlin before entering the cab.

"Hey, did you see that? A single snap of the fingers and I got a cab! I must be on a winning streak! Keep your fingers crossed for me, Caity. By the time I meet you tomorrow night, I may be seriously in love!"

He didn't wait to hear her answer, and Caitlin scowled at the rear of the departing cab. "Great," she muttered. "Just great. That's all I need to make my weekend totally perfect—Alec Woodward spending our dinner together telling me how much he loves Michelle Morreau and what a perfect wife she's going to be."

"Michelle has a wonderful sense of humor," Alec said. "And that's a really important quality in a wife, don't you think? She kept us both laughing all evening long. Did I mention that before?"

Caitlin unclenched her teeth and tried for a smile. "A couple of times, actually. You also told me she's cute, pretty, intelligent, great at her job and has a fascinating perspective on French politics." She set down her fork, no longer feeling any appetite for the chocolate torte she'd ordered for dessert.

"Sorry if I'm repeating myself, but I want to be sure you know how much Michelle and I enjoyed ourselves last night. You had a lot of reservations about using your professional skills to find me a wife, so it's important for you to know how much I appreciate your efforts. You should urge Sam to go ahead with his plans to establish a matchmaking division at Services Unlimited, Caity. You obviously have a real gift for pairing up compatible people. I knew you'd select just the right person when I asked you to help me find the perfect bride, and you haven't let me down."

"Is it settled then? Have you... have you and Michelle decided to get married? That's... that's great news. Professionally for me, I mean. And for you personally, of course...."

Caitlin snapped her mouth shut, stopping the inane babble. Her smile had been fixed rigidly in place ever since Alec had picked her up nearly three hours ago, and her jaw muscles were beginning to feel numb. The rest of her body, by contrast, was alive with feeling. Her nerve endings seemed to explode every time Alec mentioned Michelle's name.

Alec laughed easily. He'd been laughing and smiling all night long, but *his* laughter seemed entirely natural and carefree. "Hey, Michelle and I need to know each other a little better before we make such an important decision, but to be perfectly frank with you, I can hardly wait for our next meeting."

Caitlin reached for her wineglass. "And when is that going to be?"

"Tomorrow. We're going to the zoo."

Caitlin gulped down a swig of wine. "How lovely."

"She wants to see the new baby gorilla." Alec's expression softened and his voice lowered. "Michelle loves babies. She wants to have children right away, and I've realized I want that, too. As soon as possible."

"This is a rather sudden urge for instant fatherhood, isn't it?"

"Not really. The truth is, Caity, I've felt a lot of gaps in my life recently, and my career isn't going to fill any of them. I'm envious of your sister and her husband, waiting for the birth of their first child. Aren't you?"

She avoided his gaze. "In some ways, but unfortunately women have to make enormous sacrifices in order to raise a baby to adulthood."

"True, but think of the compensations! And nowadays fathers share more of the child-rearing burdens, which means women don't have to give up all their independence and abandon their careers just because they're also mothers." He took her hand and stroked it absently, running his thumb over the vein pulsing in her wrist. "I went to bed last night and lay in the darkness imagining what it feels like to watch your wife's body grow and change while she carries the child you've helped to create. I tried to imagine how it would feel to watch my wife give birth to *our* child, a living being the two of us had made together. Don't you ever wonder how it would feel to hold your very own baby in your arms, Caity?"

He was conjuring up images Caitlin rarely allowed herself to dwell on. Deciding not to marry had been easy for her, and the disastrous experiment with David had merely confirmed her decision. She'd seen what marriage meant for women, and she didn't believe the game was worth the cost. But in the darkest, deepest, most secret corner of her heart, she had never quite accepted the fact that if she didn't marry, she probably ought not to have a child. She didn't want to answer Alec's question, for it was too painful, but she also knew he deserved more from her than a flip, easy evasion.

"I held both my nephews when they were only a few hours old," she said at last. "Newborn babies have a special feel, sort of warm and solid, even though they look so fragile." She stared into her empty wineglass. "I've never felt so envious in my entire life as I did when Megan first put Zach into my arms. At that moment, I would have given almost anything to change places with my sister, to be Zachary's mother instead of his aunt."

"Zach is four," Alec said thoughtfully. "And four years ago you got engaged to David. Is there a connection?"

"Perhaps," she admitted. "But in the end, you know what happened to David and me. I told you last week. Our big mutual-confession night."

He squeezed her hand, eyes smiling. "Yeah, you told me this great sob story. But what I heard was that you and David weren't really suited to each other, and that doesn't prove anything about the long term. Take my word for it, Caity, any day now, the love of your life is going to explode onto the scene, and you'll think to yourself, Wow! This is what true love feels like. Thank heaven I wasn't dumb enough to marry good ol' Dave."

She laughed, her first unforced laugh of the evening. "When that happens, Alec, you'll be the first to know."

"I'll be waiting. In the meantime, shall we dance?"

"Dance?" She looked over toward the corner of the restaurant, where a trio of musicians played romantic tunes from the forties and fifties. Two middle-aged couples, obviously enjoying themselves, were revolving slowly around the small dance floor. She shook her head. After what happened on Monday night, the idea of stepping into Alec's arms again was...unsettling. "I'm sorry, Alec, but I need something livelier. After all, my sisters and I grew up with John Travolta and *Saturday Night Fever.* Unless there are strobe lights and hundred-decibel amplifiers, my feet won't move."

"Then I know the place for us. There's a genuine disco just around the corner from here if you'd like to go and check it out."

She looked up eagerly. "Black velvet walls, terrible drinks, and a laser light show every ten minutes or so?"

He grinned. "You've got it. Sound like your kind of place?"

"Sounds perfect. What are we waiting for?"

ALEC DREW HIS CAR to a halt in the parking lot outside
Caitlin's apartment building in Arlington. She stirred
sleepily. "Do I have to move?"

"Only if you want to get out of the car."

She yawned and forced herself to sit upright. "I suppose I'd better get some sleep."

"There's not much of the night left."

She glanced at her watch. "Four o'clock! Good grief,
no wonder I'm exhausted."

"The night went fast, didn't it?"

"Too fast. My feet are worn down to the ankles, but
that was the most fun I've had in years. How come nobody ever told me what a fantastic dancer you are?"

"My family doesn't know all my secrets," he said
lightly. "Come to that, how come nobody ever told me
you can do the splits? Not to mention back flips."

She groaned. "And I'll have the aching muscles tomorrow to prove it! Alec, you don't think we were
maybe a touch—uninhibited—during that last dance?"

He grinned. "Just because the DJ whistled and the
bartender dropped his tray of glasses? Nah—you were
great, Caity."

"I should go in. If I can find my shoes..." She
scuffed around on the floor with her toes and Alec
leaned across to pick up her sandals. "Are these what
you're looking for?"

"Yes, thanks."

"Here, let me help you put them on. It's too cold to
walk across the parking lot barefoot."

He leaned down and Caitlin found herself staring at
the back of his head while he slipped her shoes onto her
feet and buckled the straps. His dark hair curled thick
and unruly against his neck, and before she could stop
herself, her hand stretched out to touch. Her fingers

ruffled up through the springy thickness of his hair and Alec grew very still.

As soon as she realized that he'd noticed what she was doing, Caitlin snatched back her errant fingers. Alec straightened and returned to his own side of the car. "Does my hair need cutting?" he asked, his voice oddly strained.

"No, no. It's fine just like it is." *Fool!* she chastised herself silently. *If you'd agreed it was too long, you wouldn't need to find another explanation for why you were stroking his neck.*

"My hair grows fast," Alec said.

She let out her breath in a sigh of profound relief that he wasn't going to make a big deal out of her momentary aberration. "Does it? Well, anyway, thanks for a lovely evening, but I must get to bed. I've agreed to meet a friend for brunch tomorrow, and I'm going to be lousy company unless I get a few hours sleep."

"Anyone I know?"

"I don't believe so. He's an assistant curator at the Smithsonian. He's very nice."

"Ah, nice." Alec fell silent, then got out of the car and came around to open Caitlin's door. "I'll see you upstairs," he said. "I'd better make sure there are no ghoulies and ghosties waiting to attack in the corridors."

They didn't speak again until they stood in the hallway outside her apartment. Alec looked down at her, his face shadowy in the muted light. "Good night, Caity. Sleep well."

She wished she could see his expression so that she could guess what he was thinking. His mouth was very close to hers. If she tilted her chin just the tiniest fraction, he would hardly be able to avoid kissing her. But of course she wasn't interested in kissing Alec. She'd been angry at him all week precisely because last Monday he'd chosen to kiss her. Why provoke an action that made her angry? She would say good-night and leave.

Caitlin tilted her chin. Her lips touched Alec's. For a moment suspended in time he did absolutely nothing. Then his arms slowly closed around her and he drew her tight against his chest. He took her mouth in a long, passionate kiss, while his hands held her clamped against the taut, hard length of his body.

Caitlin's head spun dizzily; her veins fizzed with fire. Then her stomach knotted and the familiar fear returned, swamping her with panic. She jerked her head away, but Alec wouldn't let her go. He caught her face in his hands and lowered his head toward her. "You give such wonderful kisses," he murmured against her lips. "Kiss me, Caity. I need you to kiss me."

If she'd been smart, she'd have taken to her heels and run. If she'd been smart, she'd certainly have reminded him that he was escorting Michelle Morreau to the zoo tomorrow. But Caitlin wasn't smart. Like the fool she was, she kissed him back. And this time, she was so far gone into craziness that she wished the kiss could have lasted forever.

Finally, much too late, sanity returned. She drew back, huddling her arms around her waist. "We shouldn't have done that," she whispered. "Alec, we're friends, and friends don't exchange that sort of kiss."

"You're right," he said, his voice abstracted. "There was nothing friendly about that kiss."

She looked at Alec and, instead of the familiar boy next door, saw a dark, forceful, sexually riveting stranger. Panic washed over her in a cold, engulfing wave, and she did what she should have done five minutes earlier. She fled.

CHAPTER FIVE

CAITLIN'S DATE with Richard, the curator from the Smithsonian, had not been a success. Either because she was tired, or because she was in an unusually critical mood, she'd found his company boring in the extreme. She wondered why she'd never noticed before that he was incapable of discussing anything without dragging the conversation around to the habits of primitive tribal peoples, living in obscure corners of the globe.

"Yes, that *was* an entertaining movie," Richard had agreed, when she tried to introduce a subject that had nothing at all to do with folk customs of the world. "Some of its underlying suppositions reminded me of the Anawoponga tribe in the South Pacific. Did you know that the Anawoponga believe that murdered souls always come back to haunt their murderers?"

"No, I hadn't heard of the Anawong... Anapong..."

"Anawoponga. They're a fascinating society altogether, a unique cultural relic that Western society needs to cherish. At puberty, the males are initiated into adulthood by the medicine man..." And off he'd rattled on a ten-minute lecture on the circumcision ceremonies of the Anawoponga, to be rapidly followed by a dissertation on the burial rites of the Betuni and the religious education of the Monguyvu, a particularly obscure tribe recently discovered in the heart of the Ecuadoran rain forest.

Caitlin hadn't been required to contribute to any of these lectures, merely to nod appreciatively and listen quietly. She'd found herself wondering with increasing frequency how Alec and Michelle were enjoying themselves at the zoo. She couldn't help thinking they were having a wonderful time. Alec was such good company it was hard to imagine Michelle *not* enjoying herself. Caitlin wished she'd been lucky enough to spend the afternoon watching baby gorillas at the zoo, with Alec to share her laughter at their antics.

The telephone rang, jolting Caitlin out of her reverie and into the reality of the present, which was Monday morning at the office, a stack of phone message slips waiting to be answered and a desk drowning in paper. The phone call was from the Japanese ambassador, calling personally to say how delighted he was with Algernon Littlethwaite, his new butler, and could Services Unlimited please find him an equally splendid English nanny to take care of his grandchildren when they visited next month?

Caitlin promised the ambassador her best efforts. Screening out all errant thoughts, she managed, by dint of nonstop work, to return all her phone calls, contact three prospective nannies and reduce the pile in her "pending" tray to the point that the folders no longer toppled over if she accidentally jostled the desk.

Late in the afternoon, she was trying to decide which urgent project to tackle next when Alec walked into her office unannounced. "Dot wasn't at her desk," he explained. "Could you spare me a couple of minutes?"

"Sure, take a seat." Caitlin's breath was suddenly coming faster, and she could feel the heat flaming in her cheeks. She smiled, hoping Alec wouldn't notice anything out of the ordinary in her manner. "Today's been a good day, so I'm only about a week behind on my paperwork. What's up?"

"Slightly more chaos at the office than usual. Leon Mancuso has asked me to defend him."

"Wow! That's a biggie." Leon Mancuso was a world-famous pianist accused of murdering his mistress while his blind wife slept in a nearby bedroom. The publicity surrounding his arrest had been enormous, and Caitlin could imagine the media interest aroused by the news that Mancuso was changing defense attorneys. "Do you think you can make a decent case?" she asked.

"It isn't going to be easy, but we'll give it our best shot. Anyway, Mr. Mancuso isn't why I came. I'd like to catch you up on my news about Michelle."

Caitlin couldn't read his expression and she discovered that her heart was pumping nineteen to the dozen. Had he come to announce his wedding plans? The prospect of Alec married to Michelle Morreau produced a tumult of emotions too complex to analyze, but powerful enough to leave her feeling battered. It took a couple of seconds before she could unclench her hands and produce a smile. "I hope everything's going smoothly. How was your trip to the zoo yesterday?"

"We had a lot of fun. The better I know Michelle, the more I like her. She's really a terrific person."

Personally speaking, Caitlin hadn't found her *that* wonderful, but Alec's eyes glowed every time he mentioned the darn woman. Caitlin turned away. Alec seemed to be watching her much too closely, and she wasn't willing to have her feelings probed right at this moment. She jumped up and walked briskly across the room, closing a cabinet drawer that could just as well have remained open. When she was sure she had her voice and smile under control, she faced Alec again.

"Let me guess," she said with false cheer. "You've come to deliver your check."

"My check?"

"For professional services successfully rendered." She swallowed. "I assume you're here to announce that you and Michelle plan to get married."

She had the oddest impression that Alec was disappointed. The impression was so fleeting, however, she couldn't be sure.

"No," he said after a tiny pause. "I'm afraid we're not going to get married. In fact, I've just come from driving Michelle to the airport. At this very moment, she's taking off on the evening flight from Dulles to Paris."

"To Paris! Why is she going there? Good grief, she only just flew back to the States a couple of weeks ago!"

Alec's familiar grin returned with all its insouciant charm. "I thought you'd be surprised, but her ex-husband is in Paris, you know. Tall, dark, handsome Philippe."

"Right, and that's precisely why she left. To get away from talk, dark, handsome Philippe and to put her failed marriage behind her."

"Her feelings are more complicated than that. Have you noticed that human emotions tend to be far more complex than they seem on the surface? Michelle admitted to me yesterday that she's still in love with Philippe. Madly in love, in fact."

"What? She certainly didn't sound as if she cared two cents for him when I interviewed her last week."

"Maybe you didn't ask the right questions," Alec said quietly. "Remember, you were assessing her job qualifications, whereas I was trying to understand her as a person. Besides, I've been in a similar situation myself, and so it was easy for me to recognize the signs of a woman still deeply involved with her former husband. I suspected something of how Michelle felt on Friday night, and by the time we'd spent a couple of hours together on Sunday, I was sure of it."

Good heavens, what a mess, Caitlin thought. Why in the world hadn't Michelle discovered she was still in love with her ex-husband before she started to date Alec? And yet, even as she posed the question in her mind, Caitlin realized she wasn't entirely surprised by the news. Past experience with friends and acquaintances suggested that this was precisely the sort of weird behavior typical of people in the throes of love and passion. Never having been in love herself, Caitlin was constantly amazed by the emotional tangles lovesick people got themselves into.

In the meantime, while Michelle winged off to Paris, Caitlin was left behind to sort out the mess. She hoped Alec wasn't seriously disappointed by his failure to make a match with Michelle, although she suspected this must be why she'd seen his expression darken into that earlier look of fleeting disappointment. He must be suffering the pain of dashed hopes and wounded feelings. Thank goodness the relationship between the pair of them hadn't really had time to develop into anything truly serious.

"Oh, Lord, I'm sorry," she murmured, returning to her desk. "What a horrible letdown for you, Alec. If I'd suspected any of this, I'd never have arranged your initial meeting. The last thing I intended was to reopen painful memories of your experience with that woman you loved.''

"I don't have painful memories, Caity, so don't blame yourself for something that didn't happen. I fell in love with a woman who didn't return my feelings, but I don't regret the experience one bit. Loving someone is always worthwhile.''

His words carried the ring of truth, and Caitlin, with relief, set aside her guilt. Then the full impact of his news burst over her, and she realized with a little shock of delight that Alec wasn't going to get married, after all. A heavy burden lifted from her shoulders, a burden she hadn't been aware of carrying until it disappeared. The stiff smile she'd kept pasted to her lips changed into one of genuine warmth, and she leaned back in her chair, ready to relax.

"I'll be honest with you, Alec. I'm really happy that your relationship with Michelle didn't develop into anything more serious. I'm pleased she's going to give her marriage to Philippe another try, and I'm even more pleased that you aren't going to marry her."

He chuckled. "Aha! Now we get to the real truth. Come on, confess, Caity. You were jealous of Michelle because you always planned to marry me yourself. Not right now, of course, but in ten years or so, when your biological clock ticked right down to the last possible moment.''

Caitlin stared at him blankly, then saw his eyes sparkle with laughter. Surely that meant they were back on their old footing. He was teasing her, just the way he always did.

"Hey, you found me out. Now, shall we get serious for a few minutes? After your experience with Michelle, I'm sure you want to call off this crazy deal with our company to find you a wife. Since Services Unlimited never completed our part of the contract, I'm more than willing to return your fees. I suggest we bill you strictly for office overhead and expenses incurred so far. Does that sound fair?''

"More than fair. Except what makes you think I'm ready to call it quits? I want to get married, and your company promised to introduce me to at least four prospective brides. So far I've only met one."

"You don't plan to continue with this ridiculous search? Alec, you *can't* mean to continue."

"Why not? My needs remain the same as they were when we first talked about this. I want to marry as soon as possible, and I need help in finding a suitable partner. Just because Michelle and I aren't rushing to take out a marrige license doesn't mean I've given up on the idea of finding a wife with your professional help."

Caitlin discovered that, for some obscure reason, she was starting to feel angry. "Fine," she snapped. "When I come across a suitable candidate, I'll let you know. However, custom-designed brides are in scarce supply, and I should warn you that the average age of job applicants interviewed by this company is forty-three. So don't expect a stream of luscious young nubiles to be wafting your way any time soon."

Alec stood up, appearing totally unruffled by her peevish tone. "I'm not looking for a luscious young nubile. I want a mature woman, willing to take the risk of committing herself to a serious relationship."

"I'll keep your requirements in mind."

"Thanks." He smiled blandly. "Remember, I'm paying your company a hefty fee for this service, and finding me a wife is your best bet for promotion if you want to be a vice president by Christmas."

"Prospective wives don't grow under cabbages," she muttered.

He grinned and began moving toward the door. "No, that's babies. Didn't your mother teach you anything?" He gave her a friendly wave, then stopped abruptly in the doorway. "I almost forgot. I need a favor, Caity. I have to take the president of Ergon Industries out to dinner tonight, and he's bringing his wife. Would you be an angel and come with us? I need a warm female body to even up the numbers."

"Hey, what a flattering invitation."

"Okay, I need a warm, beautiful and intelligent female body to even up the numbers. How's that?"

"Too little too late. Anyway, I have a lot of work to catch up on—"

"We're not meeting till eight, and you could come straight to the restaurant if you like. The Pear Tree—it's one of your favorites—and since you have to eat dinner, you may as well eat somewhere nice. Besides, I need your company tonight. I'm feeling depressed and rejected now that Michelle has left me—"

"All right, quit with the sob story—you've talked me into it." Caitlin pulled a bulging file toward her. "Now go away, Alec, or I'm going to be fired by Christmas, not promoted to VP."

He gave a mock salute. "Yes, ma'am. See you at eight."

Caitlin refused to think about Michelle's defection to Paris or Alec's absurd insistence on interviewing more candidates for the role of wife. She couldn't afford to waste the time. For a solid hour she worked with robotlike efficiency, setting up interviews, checking references and drafting letters. At five-thirty, Dot stuck her head into the office to say goodbye. The building grew quiet and Caitlin's pace of work picked up. This part of the day was often her most productive time, and she had no intention of blowing it by allowing her mind to wander.

She was concentrating so hard she literally jumped in her chair when Dot suddenly burst back into the office, eyes gleaming with the light of battle. "Sam's on his way," she announced. "No time to explain, but I'm warning you, Caitlin, whatever he says, just keep answering no. I'm going to bring that man to his senses if it's the last thing I do."

"I thought you'd left."

"I would have if I'd been smart. Sam asked me to help him with a special project, and one thing led to another. Psst, here he comes."

Sam strolled into the office. Dark suit immaculate, silver hair neatly brushed, he bore little resemblance to the frazzled father who had begged a ride to the airport the previous Friday.

"Caitlin, how's it going?" His smile was so wide she knew Dot was right. Sam was up to something. He favored the no-nonsense approach unless he was planning something outrageous.

"Busy. But I guess that's good."

"Business is brisk at the moment, that's for sure, but you've had too many projects pushed onto your desk recently. I feel guilty about the amount of overtime you're putting in."

"I don't mind."

"I know you don't, but I've no interest in turning my employees into slave laborers, so you'll be pleased to hear that I've hired some extra help. Remember that candidate I asked you to chat with a couple of weeks ago? José Menendez?"

"I liked him a lot, as I told you. He seemed well qualified, and a nice, coolheaded guy to boot. That's always a definite plus when things heat up around here."

"I agree, and his final reference came in today. Everything checked out fine, so I've offered him a job as a recruiter."

"Great! I'm sure his special expertise in hiring Hispanic workers will be very valuable for us."

"Yes, and apparently he's a real whiz at unsnarling visa problems."

Caitlin eyed her boss. "We went over all this after the initial interviews, Sam. You may as well tell me what's really on your mind. This facade of sweet reason isn't getting you anywhere, because Dot's already blown the whistle on you. You didn't come in here to tell me about José Menendez."

"Hah!" Sam swung around to glare at Dot, who was standing in the doorway, arms crossed. She glared right back. "I might have known you couldn't be trusted to keep a secret," he spluttered.

"How can your crazy plan be a secret from Caitlin?" Dot demanded. "You're expecting her to put it into action."

"It's not a crazy plan. It's brilliant strategic thinking!" Sam's cheeks puffed out in annoyance, but since it was the start of the week, a safe four days from the loneliness of Friday night, he quickly regained control of his temper.

"I have a new client for your matrimonial-services division," he said to Caitlin, with another wide smile that didn't quite cover his nervousness.

"A man?" Caitlin asked, wondering if Sam planned to suggest himself as a client. He struck her as the sort of man who needed a wife, not to mend his socks or cook his dinner, but to fill the emptiness of his evenings and add color to the drabness of his weekends. "Is this new client a friend of yours?" she prompted tactfully.

"It's not a man," Sam said. "It's a girl—"

"Woman," Dot interrupted. "Jodie is a *woman*, Sam, not a girl, and that's what you keep forgetting."

"Girl, woman, what's the difference? Anyway, I want Caitlin to fix her up with that lawyer fellow. Send them out on a date and see what comes of it."

"Jodie has agreed to be taken on as a matrimonial client?" Caitlin asked, stunned. "When did she decide she wanted to get married? I thought she was planning to go to Africa for a year of postgraduate work in environmental biology."

"That's exactly what she's planning," Dot said.

"She's planning nothing of the kind!" Sam roared. He swallowed hard and his expression became pleading. "She doesn't know what she wants," he assured Caitlin. "If she could just find the right man, I know she'd settle down and get married in a shot."

Caitlin didn't even bother to dispute this dubious premise. "Well, Sam, I'm sorry, but I don't see how I can help you. As you know, Alec Woodward is the only client on our books at the moment—"

"And he would be perfect for my little girl!" Sam declared triumphantly.

Caitlin wondered if she had heard right. "Sam, Alec's almost thirty-five years old, a sophisticated man about town. Jodie's barely twenty-two, and still trying to grasp the alien concept that there's a whole world outside the confines of the lab and her test tubes."

"A dozen years' age difference, that's nothing, and Alec would soon teach her what's what. Besides, I read his file over the weekend, and he sounds like just the sort of man I want for a son-in-law. Hardworking, successful, healthy, well-rounded..." He trailed off. "You've known him for years—there's nothing wrong with his health or his background, is there, Caitlin?"

"No, but—"

"It's settled, then. I'll bring Jodie into the office tomorrow and you can fix her up with this fellow."

"Fine," Caitlin said. "I'll do that. As soon as Jodie comes into my office and gives me all the pertinent details, I'll arrange a date with Alec."

Sam beamed in satisfaction. "Tomorrow," he said. "She'll be here first thing." He cast Dot a look of unconcealed triumph. "I'm glad some people in this office have functioning brain cells," he declared.

"Right," Dot agreed. "It's a pity you're not one of them."

Sam bristled, but he didn't deign to reply. As soon as he left the office, Dot walked over to Caitlin's desk. "You aren't really planning to set Jodie up with Alec Woodward, are you, Caitlin? My Lord, the poor kid doesn't need you hounding her, as well as her father."

"Of course I'm not planning to set her up with Alec, but there was no point in upsetting Sam."

"Why not? That's his problem. Since his wife died, everyone humors him, instead of telling him point-blank when he's making a total ass of himself."

"Maybe you're right. But what are the chances of Jodie's agreeing to come into the office and get her name entered into our books? One in a million?"

Dot didn't look reassured. "You don't understand. Sam will keep nagging at her until she says yes."

Caitlin didn't know Sam's daughter well, but she'd met her often enough to suspect that she would beat out any mule in a competition for stubbornness. The more Sam nagged, the more likely Jodie would be to dig in her heels and refuse to budge. But since Dot looked really worried, Caitlin tried to reassure her.

"In my opinion, Jodie and Alec wouldn't enjoy each other's company, so even if Jodie comes to see me, I can simply recommend against a meeting. That would be a professional judgment on my part, and Sam wouldn't question it. Give him his due—once he trusts an employee's professional skills, he never second-guesses business decisions. Jodie isn't going to get pushed into a relationship with Alec Woodward, even if Sam *does* own this company."

"You make it sound so simple."

"That's because it is simple. Trust me on this one, Dot. Jodie will be on her way to Africa right after the holidays, just like she planned."

"And where will Alec Woodward be?"

"Living the bachelor life here in Washington, I guess."

"With those looks and that personality?" Dot picked up her coat. "Sometimes I wonder where supersmart women like you park their brains after office hours."

Caitlin laughed. "What does that cryptic comment mean?"

"Stick around, honey, and maybe you'll find out."

CHAPTER SIX

CHARLIE KERRICK and his wife, Brenda, turned out to be fascinating people, and Caitlin was glad she'd accepted Alec's invitation to join them for dinner. Charlie had inherited a small engineering company from his uncle when he was barely out of college. Now, some thirty years later, he'd successfully turned Ergon Industries into a major manufacturer of tool-and-die equipment, headquartered in Pittsburgh, but with interests and subsidiaries all over the world.

The Pear Tree was a restaurant conducive to relaxed conversation, and over a meal of shrimp Creole followed by lemon soufflé, Charlie explained to Caitlin that he was in Washington to discuss the opening of Ergon offices in several former Communist countries.

"I want to help rebuild the economies of Eastern Europe," he said. "My mother's family immigrated to the States from Poland right before the Second World War, so I feel a real attachment to the place. I even understand a few words of Polish, which helps a bit when I'm over there, talking to the people who might like to work for me one day. But I'm dealing with stockholders' money, so I have to think like a businessman, not like a philanthropist, and the harsh economic reality is that conditions in much of Eastern Europe are still too unsettled for capitalist enterprises to be commercially successful."

"Somehow, I don't think that's going to stop you from rolling up your sleeves and pounding the pavement until you find a way to make the investment profitable," Alec said. "You get a gleam in your eye every time you say the word 'Poland.'"

His wife laughed. "So you've noticed that, too? I think we'll be living in Krakow or Warsaw some time within the next six months. Fortunately our youngest child started college last year, so I'm already packing my bags and figuring out how many pieces of paper I'll need from various government departments before I can get myself licensed to practice medicine over there."

"Alec never mentioned you're a doctor," Caitlin said, a little surprised by the news, partly because Brenda looked so much like the typical suburban homebody.

"I'm a dermatologist, with a subspeciality in childhood skin diseases. I met Charlie while I was in medical school and decided he was too good a catch to let go."

Her husband bowed. "Thank you, dear."

"Don't get swollen-headed. I might change my mind any day now." She flashed him a smile that showed he had absolutely no need to worry. "When Charlie persuaded me to get married, I had to change my career plans just a little," she continued. "I'd intended to become an obstetrician, but that's a very demanding speciality, since babies have a perverse habit of deciding to be born at three in the morning, or in the middle of Thanksgiving dinner, or some other totally inconvenient time."

"Our son was born on my brother's wedding day," Charlie remarked. "Four weeks early."

"At least he started the way he planned to go on!" Brenda said. "He's never had a lick of patience from that day to this." They both smiled fondly, exchanging a look Caitlin had seen many times on her sister's face when her sons, Zach and Matt, did something outrageous, such as planting their toy trucks in a flower bed to see if they would grow. Parents, she decided not for the first time, loved their children for the oddest of reasons.

"How did you manage to cope with raising a family and being a full-time doctor?" she asked, genuinely curious.

"I didn't always work full-time," Brenda explained. "I couldn't see much point in producing babies who would be raised by nannies, which is what would have happened if I'd specialized in obstetrics. On the other hand, I'd sweated blood getting through medical school, and it seemed criminal to throw away so much training and education. So I decided to forget about being an obstetrician and became a dermatologist, instead."

"I can see that dermatologists aren't likely to have many emergencies," Caitlin said.

"Almost none, thank heaven. Once I got through my residency, I was able to find a practice willing to hire me part-time, and I didn't begin working forty-hour weeks until the kids were in junior high. Now Charlie is burned out and getting ready to retire, and I tell him I'm just getting into my stride. For the next twenty years, when we come back from Poland, he can stay home and cook supper while I climb the professional ladder."

Caitlin didn't need to ask if Brenda was satisfied with the choices she'd made; both she and Charlie radiated contentment with their lives and with each other. Some women might not approve of the compromise the Kerricks had worked out, but Caitlin thought they'd achieved a fair balance. True, Charlie had forged ahead building his industrial empire while Brenda made all the career changes and sacrificed her personal goals to keep the home front afloat. But would Brenda have been happier if she'd rejected Charlie and stuck to her original dream of becoming an obstetrician? Caitlin was sure of the answer to that question. Brenda's face glowed with affectionate pride when she mentioned her three children, and her eyes softened every time she glanced at her husband. Brenda was obviously a woman who felt truly fulfilled.

Caitlin said as much to Alec as he drove her home. "Brenda and Charlie have been lucky," he agreed. "But I think most couples are likely to have a harder time juggling their careers and their personal lives than those two did."

"I expected you to hold Brenda over my head as an example of how easy it is nowadays for a woman to combine a career with marriage and motherhood."

He smiled. "Then I'm glad I'm not a hundred percent predictable."

She could have told him that for the past two weeks she'd found him about as predictable as a tiger deciding whether to target a deer or an antelope for his supper, but she decided not to say anything that might spoil the rapport they'd finally managed to reestablish. "Want to come in for a cup of coffee?" she asked. "It's only ten-thirty."

Alec looked wary, and she laughed. "Don't be afraid—it's safe to say yes. Richard, the guy who took me out to brunch yesterday, gave me a present of real coffee beans from a fancy boutique in Georgetown. He brought a tiny bottle of whiskey and some whipping cream, too. We could make Irish coffee.''

"Clearly a smart man if he's already discovered that he needs to bring his own coffee supplies when he visits you."

Caitlin grinned, not in the least offended. "Smart, kind and a total bore. Believe me, I envied you and Michelle yesterday, watching baby chimps at the zoo."

He shot her a peculiar sideways glance as he parked the car. "Want to come to the zoo with me next weekend? There's another chimp expected to give birth any hour now. We might get to see a newborn."

"I'd love that." She was surprised at how pleased she felt at the prospect of spending an entire afternoon in Alec's company. Surprised, because there had been so much tension between them ever since he'd announced his plans to marry. But it was getting late, and she felt agreeably sleepy, so she smiled at him, not wanting to destroy her good mood with too much analysis. "Are you coming in now that you know the coffee's safe to drink?''

"Sure." He held the door open so that they could walk into the lobby of her building. "Although it's depressing to think my chief role in your life is as a human coffee percolator."

She shook her head with mock severity. "Not the *chief* role, Alec. There are other things you do that I value more."

"Name one."

"There must be something, although making great coffee is a major talent of yours." She yawned and pressed the button to summon the elevator. "It's too late at night for serious conversation. Trust me, Alec, you're the most important man in my life."

The words slipped out, and she would have called them back if she could. Fortunately Alec chose not to make any comment. Perhaps he didn't realize how revealing her bantering remark was, but Caitlin knew she'd inadvertently spoken the truth. Alec *was* the most important man in her life, and she was going to feel devastated when he married. She felt like a complete dog in the manger where he was concerned. She didn't want another woman to become the focus of his attention and she couldn't bear to contemplate a wife usurping her position as Alec's best friend.

But his marriage still lay in the future, maybe even far in the future. Tonight it seemed that Alec was willing to return to his familiar friendly role, and Caitlin felt her happiness blossom. They joked around with easy camaraderie while he brewed coffee in her tiny neat kitchen. Then she poured generous servings of Irish whiskey into the bottom of two cups and topped the steaming coffee with scoops of sweetened whipped cream. Alec carried the mugs into the living room, searching for coasters while she rummaged around for the package of family photos that had arrived in yesterday's mail from her mother.

Finding the photos, she kicked off her shoes and curled up against the soft, plum-colored cushions of her sofa. Alec tossed his jacket onto a chair and sprawled at the opposite end of the same sofa, chuckling as he admired shots of Zach and Matt creating toddler mayhem in their backyard sandbox.

"I saved the best till last," Caitlin said, holding up a grainy black-and-white snapshot. "Take a look at this."

Alec stared in silence at the blur of gray shadows. "What's it supposed to be?" he asked, twisting the photo to various angles. "It looks like a close-up of static electricity on your parents' TV set."

She laughed. "You thought that, too? Which just shows how ignorant we both are. That, my dear Alec, is a picture of my new niece- or nephew-to-be. Mom insists it's a wonderfully clear ultrasound picture of Merry's new baby."

Alec gave the snapshot another concentrated examination, then grinned. "Yeah, I can see it's a really cute baby. One problem. Is it a boy or a girl?"

"Even Mom and the doctor can't tell that detail yet, but everyone agrees the baby is perfect in every way— right size, perfectly formed spinal cord, arms and legs in place, fingers and toes all present and correct."

"Why did Merry have the ultrasound, or is it routine nowadays?"

"Pretty much routine, I guess. But in her case there were some questions about precisely how pregnant she actually is. And it turns out she's further along than they'd first calculated. The doctor estimates the baby will arrive right at the end of March, not mid-May."

"Are Jeff and Merry pleased about that?"

"Over the moon. They only have to wait five more months to see their baby, instead of nearly seven. As far as I can tell, they're both counting the hours, not just the days."

"I have good news from home, too," Alec said. "My father's found a buyer for his hardware store, so he and my mother are having a marvelous time planning a retirement vacation. They're thinking of taking a cruise to the Bahamas."

"Alec, that's fantastic!"

"Yes, the deal looks solid, and they got a decent price."

"I'm so happy for them. I know how worried they've been, what with the economy in the doldrums and small businesses having a hard time getting bank loans." Caitlin was so pleased for her old neighbors she acted without thinking. She leaned across the sofa and flung her arms around Alec's neck, hugging him exuberantly.

Too late, she realized she'd made a serious mistake. Because of the way they'd both been sitting, she ended up crowded breast to hip against Alec's side, her thigh thrust intimately against his. Through the thin silk of her blouse she could feel the hard muscle of his chest pressing against her body, and her heart leapt—with anticipation?—as he slowly closed his arms around her waist. He didn't speak, just held her, looking at her searchingly.

For a moment frozen in time, neither of them moved. Then Alec pulled away, jumping up from the sofa and striding toward the kitchen. He paused in the doorway, turning around to give her a cheerful smile. "I'll make a fresh pot of coffee," he said. "We don't want to find ourselves exchanging any more of those hazardous, nonfriendly kisses, do we?"

"What? Oh, no, of course not. I don't know what's come over us recently."

"It's called sex," he said dryly. "It can happen to anyone, even to friends."

Fortunately he started running water into the coffee-pot before Caitlin needed to come up with a reply. She collapsed against the sofa cushions, her body shaking. *This is ridiculous,* she thought. *What's happening to me? He didn't even kiss me, so why am I getting all hot and bothered?*

Because she *wanted* him to kiss her. The unwelcome answer slipped into her mind too quickly to be pushed aside. With some reluctance, Caitlin acknowledged the appalling truth. Irrational it might be, but she did want Alec to kiss her. She wanted to recapture the magic she'd found in his arms. She wanted him to fold her into his embarace and hold her tight against his body. She wanted him to twist his fingers into her hair and hold her head captive while he teased her lips into a heated response. She wanted to lie next to him, clinging to him, skin to skin, body to body. Most of all, she wanted to feel the throb of her own desire reflected in the hot, passionate demand of his touch.

She knew exactly what she wanted, what she needed—and the knowledge sent the fear surging back.

Alec threatened everything she had carefully mapped out for her future, everything that would make her life different from that of her sisters. Her career, her independence, her freedom, would all vanish if she let herself fall in love. And Alec was especially dangerous to her plans because she found him so attractive and liked him so much. If she once allowed herself to make love to him, the experience would be so intense she suspected she would never willingly let him go. She must take care and watch her feelings, or they would race out of control. Then her happiness would be in Alec's hands, her destiny in his keeping.

The prospect of such deep and overwhelming love would be scary enough even if she was sure that Alec returned her feelings. But in fact, she had no reason to suppose he did love her. She'd just turned eight when he moved into the house next door, and he had already been fourteen, a freshman in high school. He was naturally kindhearted and he'd tolerated her tagging along on fishing trips and family vacations, but for years she'd been nothing more to him than the bratty little kid who was best friends with his sister.

Their relationship had changed when she started college. She'd come to Georgetown University, where Alec was just finishing his law degree, and somehow the age difference hadn't seemed nearly so important when she was eighteen and he was almost twenty-five. They'd gradually become friends, and that friendship had deepened over the years, becoming more important to both of them, until they'd ended up as each other's best friend.

And that's what they still were. Just friends. Even now, when he'd decided to search for a wife, Alec hadn't considered asking Caitlin if she was interested in taking on the job. Of course, she would have rejected him outright, but it would have been nice to be *asked*.... In fact, now that she thought about it, Alec's attitude toward her was positively insulting. How could he choose to date perfect strangers in preference to Caitlin, a woman he'd known and liked for practically a lifetime?

True, his thoughts and feelings recently had been less than totally clear to her. And they had shared those utterly amazing kisses. But Alec probably hadn't found those kisses as earth-shattering as she had. On the contrary, tonight when they'd hovered on the brink of another passionate embrace, he'd simply walked away and announced he'd like more coffee!

"That's a ferocious frown," Alec said, strolling back into the living room, a coffee cup in each hand. "I'll drink fast and get out of here before you throw me out on my ear."

"If you want to leave, just say so," Caitlin snapped. "There's no need to use my frowns as an excuse."

He set the cups on the table and looked at her without a trace of his usual teasing humor. "Caitlin, if you're angry with me, will you tell me why?"

She shook her head. "I'm not angry at you, Alec."

"Then what's the problem? You sure look angry."

"Not angry. I think . . . I'm confused."

"What about?"

She looked up at him, at the man who was exerting this uncomfortable, sexual tug on her senses, at the man who was also her closest friend. "I don't know," she admitted wryly. "I'm so confused, I don't even know what I'm confused about."

"Maybe things will seem easier to understand in the morning."

"I sure hope so."

He touched her lightly on the arm, and her muscles tensed in immediate, frustrating reaction. He didn't say anything, just moved a little farther away. "I'll give you a call sometime next week," he said. "Thanks for helping me entertain the Kerricks."

"Thank you for inviting me. They're a delightful couple." She flushed. "I'm sorry, Alec. I sound so stilted. I don't know why."

"Forget it. Neither of us seems to be at our best tonight." He ran his hand through his hair in a gesture that spoke of sudden, intense weariness. "Good night, Caity. I'll see myself out. Don't forget to lock the door after me."

The silence after he left was appalling. Caitlin carried their empty coffee cups out to the kitchen and tried to wash them. She broke both saucers before she decided it would be smart to leave the tidying up until

later, when her fingers might prove a bit more cooper-
ative. She was almost grateful when the ring of the telephone interrupted the chaotic whirligig of her
thoughts.

She picked up the phone. "Hello."

"Caitlin, this is Jodie Bergen."

It took a second or two for the name to register, a
split second more to register that this was a very late
hour for Sam's youngest daughter to be calling.
"Jodie, how are you? Nothing's wrong, I hope?"

"I'm at the hospital." Jodie was normally a vivacious young woman, with a bubbly, breathless way of
speaking. Tonight her voice sounded dull and heavy,
drained of energy and life.

"Has there been an accident? Are you hurt? In-
jured?"

"Not me. Daddy. He got sick right after dinner. The
doctors think he's had a mild heart attack. They're
checking him out now."

"Jodie, I'm so sorry. I'll come right over. Which
hospital are you at?"

"Georgetown University, but you don't have to
come, Caitlin. That isn't why I called."

"No, I'll come. I want to see Sam. Besides, you
shouldn't have to wait alone—"

"Thanks, I appreciate the offer, but my brother-in-
law is on the staff here, and my sister and brother are
both here with me. Dad's going to be fine, but he's not
allowed visitors right now. We're trying to keep his
anxiety level down so that he can get some rest, but the
doctors say he's worrying about his schedule tomorrow
at the office and he won't relax. Apparently he has the
entire day filled with interviews and appointments. To

be honest, I called chiefly so I can tell my father you've taken charge at work and everything is under control.''

"Everything will be under control," Caitlin promised. "I'll call his secretary—"

"That's just it. Sylvia left town on Friday to go to her twenty-fifth high-school reunion. Remember? She's out of the office for the next week."

"How could I have forgotten! She's spent six months tormenting us with her diet while she prepared for the occasion. But even with Sylvia gone, there's still nothing for Sam to worry about." Caitlin devoutly hoped she wasn't lying. "I'll call Dot, *my* secretary, and make sure she comes in early. Between the two of us, we'll soon have everything taken care of."

"Thank you. I appreciate your help."

"I wish there was something more I could do." Caitlin paused for a moment, wondering how she could find out the seriousness of Sam's condition without upsetting his daughter. She framed her question carefully. "How long is Sam likely to be in the hospital, do you know?"

"They won't say. It seems this is the second heart attack he's had. He didn't tell anyone in the family about the first one." Jodie's voice sounded even flatter than before, and Caitlin realized that the poor girl was struggling to avoid breaking down completely. The lack of color in her voice was caused by too much emotion, not an absence of it.

"Sam will be fine, Jodie," she said, wishing she felt as confident as she sounded. "Gosh, your dad is as tough as army-boot leather, and it's going to take more than a little heart trouble to keep him down. He'll be yelling at the doctors and reorganizing the nurses' workstation before you can say Jack Robinson."

"His family's very important to him," Jodie said, not really responding to Caitlin's comments. "Since my mother died...I don't know..." Her voice trailed away into uncertainty. "Someone else is waiting to use the phone, so I should hang up, but I'm planning to come into the office tomorrow, if that's all right with you, Caitlin."

"Of course! I'll prepare a summary sheet for your father, Maybe that will reassure him we've taken care of all the urgent work waiting on his desk. Tell him tonight, and perhaps it will help to ease his mind."

"I'll tell him right away. Would three o'clock be a convenient time for us to meet?" Jodie asked. "I think I'll need about a half-hour, if you can spare it."

"Three o'clock will be fine." Caitlin mentally juggled her already hectic schedule. "And give Sam my love," she added. "Tell him I'll be in to see him as soon as they allow visitors."

"I'll do that. See you tomorrow afternoon." Jodie sounded marginally more cheerful, as if her load of worry had been lightened just by sharing it.

"Call anytime if you think of some way I can help," Caitlin said.

"Thanks, but I hope I won't have to. You've already helped a lot."

Caitlin wasn't sure *how* she'd helped, but she was glad Jodie seemed more upbeat. Hanging up the phone, she glanced at her watch and saw it was barely eleven-thirty. At ten-thirty, she'd been inviting Alec to come in for a cup of coffee. Good Lord, she felt as if she'd survived about a year's worth of emotional drama during the past hour.

Still, the extra pressure looming at work wasn't all bad. Worrying about Sam, calling Dot, getting ready for bed, setting her alarm for an extra-early start in the morning, she was almost able to put Alec out of her mind.

Almost.

CHAPTER SEVEN

THE NEXT DAY, Caitlin plumbed new depths in the meaning of the word "busy." She and Dot both arrived at the office promptly at seven, but by lunchtime, despite nonstop work and a lot of help from their colleagues, they were barely managing to stay afloat. Talking into the phone at the same time as she tried to read and sign a contract prepared by a relatively new employee, Caitlin began to feel overwhelmed by the sheer volume of work. Her heart sank when a short, swarthy, handsome man came into her office, smiling as if he expected to be welcomed.

She ended her phone conversation, trying not to sound too abrupt, and scrawled her signature on the contract, which she devoutly hoped was as standard as it looked. Then she walked around her desk to greet the newcomer.

"José," she said, extending her hand and managing a weak smile. "José Menendez. How, um, nice. Were we expecting you today?"

"Sam asked me to stop by and fill out a few routine papers—tax forms, health insurance, that kind of stuff. The receptionist told me Sam was in the hospital, so I decided to let you know I was available. I figured you might be able to use some help, even though I'm not officially slated to start until next week."

"We sure do need help," Caitlin said. "But to be honest, I don't have time to show you where to get started."

"No problem. I'll just pitch in where I'm needed—someplace where I can't make too many mistakes. At least I could answer the phone and take messages."

Caitlin didn't see how José could screw up too much just answering phones, and he had seemed an extremely capable young man at their interview. She smiled at him in gratitude. "If you're willing to pick up the slack for a few hours, it would be terrific. I knew you were going to be a great colleague, José. I just didn't know how great."

He smiled back. "Wait until I've been here a couple of weeks, then you'll be truly stunned."

José proved a godsend. The number of phone calls switched through to her office tapered off almost at once, and Caitlin found she could make time to draw up a coherent roster, assigning Sam's commitments to other staff members, saving only the really complex meetings for herself. She worked solidly for a couple of hours, barely glancing up from her papers until José returned to her office carrying a plate of chocolate-chip cookies, together with a cup of lemon tea for her and a mug of aromatic black coffee for Dot.

"Wendy tells me this is what you both like to drink at this hour of the afternoon," he said, carefully moving files and setting the tray on Caitlin's credenza.

Dot sipped her coffee and rolled her eyes in ecstasy. "Heavens, it's perfect! José, where have you been all my life? Until you brought this, I hadn't realized I was about to faint for lack of nourishment."

"José, this is wonderful," Caitlin agreed, sipping her tea and feeling the knot in the pit of her stomach start to dissolve. She'd been dangerously strung out and should have realized she needed a break. "Have you taken any phone calls I ought to know about?"

"Three inquiries from job applicants. I arranged to interview them next week when we're more caught up on things. Half a dozen inquiries about Sam's health, which I answered with the latest bulletin from the hospital and the assurance he'd be back in the office soon. A furious call from a chef we placed with a senator last month. He claims he's quitting because the senator only wants to eat hamburgers. Plus we had inquiries from a couple of potential new customers for our janitorial services. I've taken all the details and I'll give you the files tonight. As far as I can tell, I haven't seriously messed up so far."

"It sounds like you've done a fantastic job," Caitlin said, finishing her cookie. "What did you tell the furious chef?"

"That we'd try to find him another position where his creative genius would be appreciated. He's coming in tomorrow. Since he's been through our company's system before, I figured he would be a relatively easy client to take care of."

Dot gave a bark of cynical laughter. "Chefs are never easy," she said. "Trust me, they make mad scientists and crazy artists look like normal people."

José smiled, but didn't appear too worried. "I'll give him my grandmother's secret recipe for quesadillas. That ought to get him onside. Which reminds me, speaking of chefs, there's a fax for you, Caitlin, from somebody called Michelle Morreau in Paris. She apologizes for not keeping her appointment in Chevy Chase with the member of cabinet, but she was busy getting married."

"*What*?" Dot shot out of her chair, cookie crumbs flying in all directions. "Alec Woodward married Michelle Morreau? In Paris, France? I don't believe it!"

Caitlin wondered why Dot sounded so totally astonished. "Calm down," she said. "Michelle didn't marry Alec. She remarried Philippe, her ex-husband."

Dot collapsed back into her chair. "Remarried? Huh, what a fool! At least I never got that stupid. Poor Michelle. If Philippe didn't appreciate her the first time around, why would he get smart the second time?"

"Some of us do learn from our mistakes," José suggested.

"Not men," Dot said. "They just get more stubborn. Look at Sam. He's known for six months—" She stopped abruptly. Looking as close to flustered as Caitlin had ever seen her, she returned her coffee mug to the tray. "Well, I guess it's back to the salt mines for all of us. I swear the pile on my in-tray gets higher the harder I work."

"And I'd better check the phone messages at the switchboard," José said. "I'll get rid of this," he added, picking up the tray and leaving the room.

"How did we ever survive without him?" Caitlin remarked, after he'd passed out of earshot. "Can you imagine? An executive who's willing to make tea and coffee—what a treasure!"

"Yeah, and his body ain't bad, either. Short, but plenty of muscle and no flab. In my book, that beats lean and lanky every time."

Caitlin laughed. "Dot, you're incorrigible. Good grief, he's twenty years younger than you!"

"So? Last I heard, window-shopping was still legal in this country." Dot went to her desk and returned with two folders. "This is the summary of today's activities you wanted typed up for Sam, and those are the letters you ought to read before you sign."

"Thanks. And I'll need the cabinet member's folder when you have a minute. With Michelle dropping out of the running, we need to find another good candidate for that position right away."

"I'll get on it now. Maybe José's disgruntled chef would be willing to do a bit of baby-sitting on the side. By the way, it's past three already. Didn't you tell me Jodie Bergen was planning to stop by about now?"

Caitlin glanced at her watch in sudden worry. "Yes, she did say that. I hope nothing unexpected happened to Sam."

"We called the hospital an hour ago. He was fine then."

As if on cue, Jodie appeared at the entrance to Caitlin's office. She looked tired, but extremely attractive, with her thick brown curls spilling out of their clip and onto her shoulders, and her slender, athletic figure shown off to advantage in a casual emerald green sweater and faded jeans.

"I met some new guy, José something. He said I should come through." She gestured to her outfit. "I'm sorry about the casual clothes. I was running late... came straight from the hospital...."

"You look fine," Caitlin said reassuringly. "We're glad you could make it."

"How's Sam?" Dot asked, sounding surprisingly curt, and Jodie seemed almost to flinch before she answered.

"He's very tired. He keeps dozing off, which isn't like him, as you know. But none of the tests so far have revealed anything really serious. The doctors say he just needs to rest and stop worrying so much about every-thing."

"May we visit him this evening?" Caitlin asked.

"Yes, anytime before nine, two visitors at a time."

"That's good news," Dot said gruffly. "Okay, I'm out of here while you two talk. I'll look up that cabinet member's file you wanted, boss."

"Why don't you sit down and relax for a moment?" Caitlin suggested to Jodie as soon as Dot left the office. "I recommend the blue chair—it's more comfortable than it looks."

Jodie obediently sat, although she perched on the edge of the chair, the picture of tension, her hands clasping and unclasping in her lap. Caitlin tried to put the young woman at ease by chatting about Sam's good test results and his uneventful recovery, but the mere mention of her father's health seemed to make Jodie even more nervous. If it hadn't been for the fact that Caitlin had conferred at length with Bruce, Sam's son-in-law and himself a surgeon, she would have begun to worry that Jodie knew something about her father's health she wasn't revealing. Having spoken to Bruce, however, Caitlin knew her boss's prognosis was about as good as it gets for a man who has suffered two minor heart attacks and still scowls at the mention of the word "exercise."

In the end, she gave up her attempts at reassurance and switched to business. Perhaps Jodie, as the only child still living at home, felt a special burden of responsibility for the handling of Sam's business affairs.

"We've already prepared a summary sheet of to-day's transactions for your father if he wants to review it," she said. "Basically we've tried to reassure him that everything here at the office is under control, and that none of his clients has been neglected. He doesn't need to read any of this material if he feels tired, but maybe he'll rest easier if he can keep his finger on the pulse of things." She handed over the file. "I've kept copies, so don't worry about losing papers. I'll bring my file when I visit Sam this evening. Please take your time reading through the material, and if you have any questions, I'll do my best to answer them."

Jodie took the folder but didn't look at it. "Actually, Caitlin, to tell you the truth, I didn't come here to talk about business. I'm not qualified to make any useful contribution, so I wouldn't dream of second-guessing your decisions. Dad trusts you completely."

"Then why did you come?"

Jodie pushed nervously at a cluster of curls tumbling across her cheek. She looked young, vulnerable and extraordinarily pretty as she plucked up the courage to speak. For a moment, seeing the lingering traces of childhood in Jodie's troubled gaze, Caitlin could almost sympathize with Sam's desire to keep this daughter, the baby of his family, home in Washington, DC, where he could protect her.

"Take all the time you need," Caitlin said. "And remember I've had a lot of experience in listening to people discuss their personal situations. That's one of the requirements of my job. So if you have a problem you think I could help solve, all you need to do is ask."

"You can help me for sure," Jodie said, then lapsed again into strained silence. With a final, impatient flick of her curls, she straightened in the chair, shoulders squaring with grim determination. She drew a deep breath. "Here goes. I would like you to arrange a date for me with Alec Woodward. I understand he's using

Services Unlimited to find him a wife, and I'd like to be considered for the position.''

Caitlin felt an instant of stunned disbelief, followed almost at once by understanding—and sympathy. ''Jodie,'' she said gently. ''You don't have to do this.''

''I know I don't have to do it. I *want* to meet Alec Woodward. It's the least I can do for Dad. . . .''

''Because your father has been so worried about you recently? Because he wants you to get married and stay here in Washington?''

Jodie kept her gaze fixed on her hands. ''Yes.''

''Guilt is a lousy reason for deciding to do almost anything, especially something as important as getting married.''

''My dad is a generous, wonderful man. I owe him.''

''Yes, you do. You owe him love and affection and respect, but not control over how you live your life.''

''I've got to do *something* to make up for all the arguments we've had recently.''

Caitlin leaned forward. ''Listen, Jodie, your father didn't have a heart attack because you want to go off to Africa next January. He got sick because his cardiovascular system wasn't functioning properly, and maybe because he didn't take proper care of his body. You're a biologist, so you should know I'm telling you the plain and simple truth.'' She smiled slightly. ''Men don't have heart attacks because their daughters argue with them, otherwise the world wouldn't be able to build enough hospitals to accommodate all the harrassed, middle-aged fathers.''

Jodie didn't crack even a tiny smile. ''Dad was showing me Alec's photo and I yelled at him, told him to stop behaving like a crazy old man. Then his face twisted into this horrible grimace of pain and he fainted.'' She looked up, cheeks paling at the memory. ''The ambulance took twelve minutes to get to our house and I was giving Dad CPR all that time. Those minutes while I waited for the paramedics to arrive were the worst twelve minutes of my whole life. I'd yelled at him—screamed at him, truthfully—and he fainted. It was cause and direct effect.''

Caitlin got up and walked across the room to put her arm around Jodie's rigid shoulders. ''Jodie, stop punishing yourself. Your father would probably have had his heart attack at the precise same instant even if you'd been discussing bridesmaids and flower arrangements for your wedding day.''

She shook her head. ''He wants me to get married. He's obsessed with the idea that I need to settle down.''

''Then your father must learn to cope with his own misguided obsession,'' Caitlin said briskly. ''You sure don't have to mess up your plans for your own life just to accommodate his harebrained vision of your future.''

''I'm twenty-two. My mother already had her first son when she was twenty-two.''

''Times have changed,'' Caitlin said. ''And even if they hadn't, there's only one valid reason to get married, and that's because you *want* to get married. Apart from anything else, have you considered this great scheme of Sam's from Alec Woodward's point of view? Can you imagine how Alec would feel, going out on a date with a woman who's offering herself up as some sort of sacrificial lamb? Come on, Jodie, get real. You're acting like the heroine in a bad Victorian melodrama, not like a sensible woman heading into the twenty-first century.''

Jodie finally gave a tiny smile, her first one of the afternoon. "A bad Victorian melodrama?" she murmured.

Caitlin grinned. "Very bad. So bad, in fact, that if you like, I'll forget you ever mentioned this nonsense about marrying Alec, and we can get right back to boring stuff like reviewing the work file I gave you earlier."

"No, as I said before, there's no reason for me to review business information you want to pass on to Dad. My specialty is the life cycle of the tsetse fly, not opportunities for profit in the employment industry."

Jodie got up and paced nervously around the room. "Caitlin, I know everything you've said about my plan to date Alec Woodward is true. At least I know *logically* that you're right. But that doesn't seem to help the way I feel. Wait until you see Dad tonight before you lecture me any more. He looks so tired, so gray and weary, as if keeping up with daily life suddenly seems more bother than it's worth." Jodie scrubbed her knuckles at the corners of her eyes and sniffed. "Damn, why don't I ever have a tissue when I need one?"

"Here." Caitlin handed her a box from the credenza. "Jodie, you're a brilliant student, a beautiful woman and a loving daughter. You don't owe your father another darn thing."

"I don't owe him, maybe, but I could choose to give him something, couldn't I?"

"Not something as crazy as a promise to marry Alec Woodward—or any other man you don't love."

"No, not marriage, maybe. But how about a date? I could tell Dad I've arranged to go out on a date with Alec Woodward, and that might cheer him up enough to make him take an interest in getting healthy again.

How about that, Caitlin?'' Jodie's cheeks grew pink with sudden enthusiasm. "Heck, who am I kidding? It's no sacrifice to go out on a date with Alec Woodward. The guy's a total hunk.''

"You sound as if you've met him,'' Caitlin said.

"Oh, no, just saw him on TV. That's what started Dad off last night, you know. They did a segment on the local TV news about Leon Mancuso and his new lawyer. Alec Woodward not only looked good enough to eat, he came up with all these witty replies when the interviewer asked him the usual dumb questions. Dad saw I was impressed, so he pulled out this folder of information about Alec. Then, of course, he couldn't understand why I didn't leap at the chance of going out on a date with the guy. Dad belongs to the generation that believes if a woman admires or likes a man, she must want to marry him.''

From the point of view of Sam's health, the idea of his daughter dating Alec wasn't totally without merit, Caitlin realized. Her stomach gave a quick, uncomfortable lurch at the thought. All her advice to Jodie so far had been solid, sincere, reasoned and from the heart. Suddenly, at the prospect of arranging a date for Jodie and Alec, she found her basic instincts at war with each other. As a professional representative of Services Unlimited she could, of course, refuse point-blank to set up the meeting. However, Sam owned the company, and after several years of working closely with him, Caitlin understood him well, and she agreed with Jodie's basic premise. In family matters, Sam was a stubborn man, with his mind set on a certain life-style for his daughter. It was likely to speed his recovery, and certainly his will to get better, if he knew Jodie was dating a man as eligible and attractive as Alec Woodward. Which was all fine and dandy—except that Caitlin was extremely unwilling to set up a meeting for the two of them.

"Alec Woodward has come to this company with a request to utilize our professional services," she said at last. "He wants to meet women who are potential marriage partners, and I don't think it would be fair or even ethical to send him out on a date with you, knowing that marriage is out of the question."

Caitlin was voicing a valid objection, but she squirmed a little in her chair, knowing she wasn't being entirely honest. Buried somewhere inside her was the fear that Jodie and Alec might find each other so congenial they would forge ahead and actually get married. And the prospect of Jodie and Alec marrying sent shivers of anxiety rippling up and down Caitlin's spine. Only because they were so unsuited, she reassured herself, not for any other, more personal reasons.

Jodie leaned forward pleadingly. "Caitlin, call him and arrange just one date for me. I promise to be honest with him as soon as we meet. I'll tell him I don't want to get married and that I agreed to the date because of Dad's state of health. We can take it from there."

"I will call Alec, but I have to tell him the truth upfront," Caitlin said after a tiny pause. "I'm not going to describe you as a serious candidate for wedding bells, because you're not."

"What will you say, then? That I want a date with him, but I'm not sure about getting married?"

"I'm going to tell him about your father's heart attack and your belief that Sam will recover more quickly if he knows you're dating Alec. That's the best deal I can offer you, Jodie. Take it or leave it."

Jodie stood up. "I'll take it. And thanks, Caitlin, for being so understanding about all this. Dad always says you're one of the few people he knows who is both clear-sighted and kindhearted. I see now why he feels that way."

The compliment was beautiful, and Caitlin wished she merited it. Right at this moment, she couldn't imagine anyone less deserving of either part of the compliment. The truth was that she didn't understand a single thing about her feelings toward Alec Woodward, and she knew for sure that her heart didn't feel nearly as much kindness toward Jodie as it should. Her cheeks grew hot, and she stood up, hoping she didn't look as embarrassed and guilty as she felt.

"Sam assumes other people share all his own good qualities," she said. "Don't count on that date with Alec Woodward, Jodie."

"I won't," Jodie said, but her sparkling eyes gave the lie to her words.

Caitlin sighed, feeling a hundred years old. "I'll try to get back in touch with you sometime tomorrow and let you know one way or the other."

"I really appreciate all your help."

"It's nothing, don't mention it." Caitlin smiled, feeling totally hypocritical. Alec, thank heaven, rarely took personal phone calls during the day, which meant she had another hour before she needed to screw up her courage and face the prospect of speaking to him for the first time since their uncomfortable parting the night before. And when they did speak, she'd have to be brisk and businesslike, convincing him how sweet and intelligent and attractive Jodie was, and how it would really be worth his while to meet her. The prospect filled her with gloom.

Two weeks ago Caitlin had thought there wasn't a subject in the world she would find difficult discussing with Alec. Over the past few days, she'd begun to wonder if the exact opposite wasn't true. Was there a single subject she and Alec could discuss without her stomach going into a nosedive and her heart starting to gallop at twice its normal speed?

Life, she decided, smothering a sigh, was sometimes very confusing.

SHE PHONED ALEC'S OFFICE at six, just before leaving to visit Sam at the hospital. Betty achieved the impossible and sounded more unfriendly than usual. Her dour response reminded Caitlin that she'd never gotten around to asking Alec why his secretary disliked her so much.

"Alec is with a client, Ms. Howard, and he has meetings scheduled until seven this evening." After four years, she showed no sign of breaking down and calling Caitlin by her first name. "The Mancuso case is exceptionally demanding."

As always, Caitlin found herself stumbling over her apologies. As always, she wondered just how Betty managed to make her feel so guilty. "I'll try him at home this evening," she said. "It's rather important, so could you tell him to expect a call around nine-thirty or ten?"

"If I must," Betty said.

It was the first time the woman had ever been flat-out rude, and Caitlin decided there would never be a better occasion to ask for an explanation of her hostility. "You know, Betty, I don't believe you're an impolite person, or an incompetent secretary, which means that you do know how to answer the phone courteously if you want to. So would you please tell me what in the world I've done to make you dislike me so much?''

There was a moment of silence during which Caitlin was sure Betty hovered on the brink of answering the question honestly. Then the moment passed, and Caitlin knew, even before the secretary spoke, that she wasn't going to tell the truth.

"I'm very sorry, Ms. Howard, I didn't intend to sound so abrupt. It's been a long day, but that's no excuse for my lack of courtesy. I was rude, and I apologize again. Please be assured that I'll pass on your message to Alec as soon as he's available. I've no doubt he'll be waiting for your call at nine-thirty this evening.''

"The perfect secretary recovers her poise," Caitlin murmured. "If you ever want to change jobs, Betty, come and see me. I'm sure I could find a great position for you. On the other hand, if you ever decide to answer my previous question truthfully, give me a call. I'd really like to know the answer.'' She hung up, hurt by the exchange even though she'd rarely met Betty and had no real reason to care if the woman had taken a dislike to her.

Her visit with Sam in the hospital did little to dispel her growing depression. Despite Jodie's warnings, she hadn't been prepared to see her feisty boss looking so ill.

"I'm not feeling as bad as I look," Sam told her with a hint of his old humor. "Here's some free advice, kiddo. Get smart and stay out of hospitals. The way they prod and poke you in this place is enough to make even a strong man feel ready to call the undertaker.''

Caitlin laughed, but the trouble was, Sam didn't look strong. Surrounded by machines, his body invaded by tubes and an IV drip, he looked downright frail. No wonder Jodie had been willing to take drastic action like dating Alec Woodward in order to boost his spirits.

She tried to interest him in cheerful anecdotes of the day's progress at the office, but she knew he wasn't really listening. Only when Dot arrived, carrying a bottle of expensive single-malt Scotch, did he perk up a little.

"This'll be waiting for you when you get out of here," she said, waving the bottle enticingly under his nose. "Jodie can drive you over to my place and I'll cook you a low-fat dinner that'll taste so good you'll think cholesterol is the chief ingredient."

"I'll drive myself!" he spluttered.

"Not if you want to eat my good food, you won't," Dot said calmly. "And for sure not if you want to have a wee dram of this whiskey."

Sam fussed and protested slightly, but after that, Caitlin was relieved to see a little color return to his cheeks and his manner no longer quite so apathetic.

Still, it hadn't been pleasant to find her ebullient boss looking so under the weather, and she found herself thoroughly depressed by the time she left the hospital. Exhaustion didn't improve her mood, either, she decided, dragging into her apartment and wondering if she had the energy to fix a bowl of soup. She wasn't hungry, but she probably needed some sustenance. Now that she thought about it, apart from an orange when she got up, and the cookie José had brought her in the middle of the afternoon, she hadn't eaten all day.

In the end, she brewed a pot of tea and toasted a slice of whole-wheat bread because that was less trouble than opening a can of soup. She still had to call Alec, and her stomach jumped nervously at the prospect of speaking to him. In two short weeks, her relationship with Alec had changed from relaxed, easygoing friendship to the point where she needed to screw up courage to pick up the phone and dial his number. *How in the world did we come to this?* Caitlin thought in bewilderment.

Procrastination was getting her nowhere. Drawing a couple of deep breaths, she picked up the phone, and punched Alec's number with nervous fingers.

He answered after the first ring, but his voice sounded tired and distracted. "Hello."

"It's Caitlin."

The pause before he responded was infinitesimal, but she heard it. "Yes, Betty told me you might call."

His voice remained flat, hovering somewhere between bored and weary. She spoke quickly, fighting an absurd impulse to burst into tears. "Sam's in the hospital. He had a minor heart attack and they're keeping him in for tests."

"I'm sorry to hear that. Sam has always seemed like a really good guy. You must be pretty busy at work."

"Very busy."

"Please give Sam my best wishes when you next talk to him."

This was awful, Caitlin thought despairingly. They sounded like two acquaintances making polite conversation because neither one of them could think of an excuse to hang up. She cleared her throat. "Betty told me how busy *you* are, so I won't keep you, Alec. In fact, this is really a business call. About your search for a wife."

Another pause, this one much longer. "Yes?" he said at last.

"Sam's daughter would like to meet you, although she doesn't want to get married right away. Her name's Jodie, and she's very young, only twenty-two—"

"I'm up to my eyeballs in depositions and pretrial motions in the Mancuso case. I don't have time to—" He broke off abruptly, then started again. "If Jodie has no interest in getting married, why does she want to meet me, for heaven's sake?"

"Her father wants to see her married and settled down," Caitlin said bluntly. "She's willing to humor him since he's in the hospital. Alec, I understand completely if you don't want to meet her."

Caitlin assumed this would be the end of the conversation. To her astonishment, she sensed Alec's interest level suddenly perk up. "You're sure she's not interested in getting married?" he asked.

"As far as I know, she's bound and determined to take off for Africa right after the New Year. She's convinced no man on earth can compete with her interest in the life cycle of the tsetse fly. If you ask her about sleeping sickness, larval worms, or other similar fascinating topics, she can talk nonstop for hours."

"We sound like ideal companions right now," Alec said, his voice containing a hint of its usual laughter. "I can drone on about briefs and depositions, while Jodie jabbers on about insects. In the meantime, Sam will be happy to know his daughter's dating a solid citizen."

"You mean you're willing to meet her?"

"Sure, why not? We can go to the movies together or something equally harmless. She needs a couple of hours away from the hospital, and I need a break from the Mancuso case."

"Well, if you're sure, I'll give her a call tomorrow."

"Why don't you give me her phone number and I'll call her myself? Since this is kind of an informal arrangement, and I already know her father, we could relax the etiquette a little, don't you agree? This way,

Jodie and I can arrange a convenient meeting spot without you having to act as go-between. Busy as you are, you could save yourself some time."

Caitlin knew Jodie would have no objections to being called directly, and Sam would be delighted to hear that things were moving so swiftly. She gave Alec the Bergens' home number, wondering why her stomach had stopped swooping and diving, only to congeal into a cold, hard knot of anxiety. Alec's behavior seemed totally out of character. He wanted a wife, so why was he willing to invite determined-not-to-marry Jodie out to the movies?

She decided to make one more attempt to clarify the situation. "You do understand that Jodie isn't willing to marry anyone right now? She wants this date with you strictly to please her father."

"I understand completely. But we'll see how things work out. You never know, she may change her mind, and I'd certainly like to help Sam over the hump."

"Well, if you're sure . . ."

"I'm sure," Alec said. "Got to go, Caity. I have a pile of paper to wade through before bedtime."

"I need an early night, too. Good night, Alec."

"Talk to you soon." He disconnected with a brisk click.

Caitlin hung up the phone and paced angrily around her apartment, stripping off her neat business clothes and tossing them over whatever piece of furniture happened to be handy. "This is crazy," she informed her TV set. "This is totally crazy."

The TV set made no comment, and Caitlin marched purposefully into her bedroom. Rummaging around in the dresser drawer for a clean nightgown, she straightened and found herself staring at a photograph of herself and Alec, taken the previous year at the Ohio State Fair. They were eating neon-pink cotton candy and were posed in front of a ferocious-looking prize bull. Alec's sexy blue eyes twinkled with laughter, and his mouth— his infuriatingly kissable mouth—seemed to invite her to come closer. The same photo had stood in the same place every day for the past fifteen months. Tonight she could hardly bear to look at it.

With a groan of frustration, Caitlin turned the photo toward the wall. Then, to her everlasting astonishment, she burst into tears.

CHAPTER EIGHT

THE REMAINDER OF THE WEEK was so busy that Caitlin's life was reduced to a survival routine of work, eat, sleep, repeat. Miraculously, late on Friday afternoon the pace seemed to slacken. Staring at her in-tray with blurry eyes, she realized that the stack of pending files had shrunk to near-normal proportions, and that there wasn't a single folder on her desk bearing an orange sticker marked Urgent.

Dot came into the office with a collection of letters requiring Caitlin's signature. "If you don't have anything too important, boss, I'm planning to leave right now and go visit Sam."

"Sure." Caitlin scrawled her signature on successive pages. "It's great that he's finally back home and perking up a bit. You have the latest office update to take to him?"

"Yes, José prepared it and he's done a terrific job. I'll tell Sam you plan to stop by tomorrow morning and catch him up on the details, right?"

"Right." Caitlin leaned back in her chair, stretching muscles that ached from too many hours hunched over her desk. "Lord, I can't remember when I last looked forward like this to the weekend. I'll be glad when Sam is fighting fit again."

"He's improving rapidly since he came home. And Jodie is certainly making him happy right now."

Caitlin yawned. "What's Jodie up to?"

Dot gave a wide smile. "Dating Alec Woodward, of course. Surely you know all about it? You set up the initial contact and they've been together every night this week. Sam's thrilled to pieces."

Caitlin realized her mouth was hanging open. She snapped it shut. "Dating? Jodie and Alec Woodward?"

Dot's smile stretched even wider. "I have to hand it to you, boss. You saw the matchmaking possibilities where those two were concerned, and the pair of them sure have hit it off."

"Wait a minute." Caitlin clutched the edge of the desk, feeling a sudden spurt of dizziness. Work this week had been so hectic she'd never followed up on the tentative arrangements Alec had made for meeting Jodie. "Dot, what are you talking about? Jodie isn't serious about Alec. She agreed to date him once, to please her father. She wanted to give Sam's recuperation a little boost, but she has no intention of getting involved in a real relationship with Alec Woodward."

Dot laughed. "Jodie may have told you she didn't intend anything serious, but that was before she met Alec in person. Honest to goodness, Caitlin, you should see the two of them together—the air positively sizzles when they hold hands! I've never seen such a couple of lovebirds in my life."

"But Jodie isn't interested in falling in love!" Caitlin protested. "She's going back to Africa. She's a scientist, obsessed with creepy-crawlies! Besides, she's only twenty-two and Alec is almost thirty-five, a very sophisticated, cosmopolitan thirty-five...."

"I guess love doesn't pay much heed to the calendar," Dot said with a sentimental sigh.

Caitlin shook her head. "Dot, listen to yourself! Since when did you get all sappy about love and romance? What's happened to the woman who three weeks ago warned me to stay smart and single."

"This is different," Dot said vaguely. "Some couples are just so right for each other even a cynic has to be touched."

"Jodie and Alec aren't suited to each other!" Caitlin said, wondering if overwork had affected her brain or everyone else's.

"Why do you sound so put out? You ought to be pleased that Alec's found a woman he likes. It's not as if you wanted to marry him yourself, is it? Anyway, I've gotta run, Caitlin. Sam isn't ready to be left alone just yet, and I know Jodie wants to go out tonight. Alec's taking her to the new play at the Lincoln Center." She waved cheerily. "Bye! See you Monday. I'll mail these letters on the way to Sam's house."

As soon as Dot left, Caitlin cleared her desk with feverish haste, stuffed a few leftover papers into her briefcase, thrust her arms into her jacket and ran for the elevator. She hailed a cab and arrived at Alec's downtown office building almost before she realized where she was heading.

The prospect of confronting the gorgon-like Betty before being admitted to Alec's office gave Caitlin no more than a few seconds' pause. Sweeping past the astonished receptionist, she stormed down the richly carpeted, oak-paneled corridor. Betty's desk sat in a screened nook directly outside Alec's office.

The secretary's pleasant smile faded to a frown as soon as she recognized Caitlin. Her greeting was chilly enough to freeze steam. "Good afternoon, Ms. Howard."

For once, Caitlin spared no time wondering why Betty looked and sounded so disapproving. "Is Alec in?" she demanded.

"He's in, but he's very busy—"

"With a client? With a partner?"

"No, not that, but he's on the ph—"

"I need to speak with him." Without waiting for permission, Caitlin knocked on Alec's door. "It's me," she said. "I have to talk to you." She pushed open the door.

Alec was on the phone. He looked up as Caitlin burst into the room, but he didn't offer his usual welcoming smile. Instead, he swiveled around on his chair, presenting her with a partial view of his profile and an excellent view of his hunched shoulders.

He laughed softly into the phone. "It's Caitlin," she heard him say. "No, I wasn't expecting her." He paused for a moment. "Right, I agree completely." His voice took on a husky tone. "Darling, this entire week has been incredible."

Darling? Caitlin's eyes were in danger of popping out of her head. She realized belatedly that this was a private phone call and that she shouldn't be listening. She walked over to the far corner of the office and tried to appear fascinated by the leather spines on a collection of law books.

Alec's conversation became more muffled, but she couldn't help hearing the throaty chuckle that marked its ending. "Bye, darling. I can hardly wait to see you." He made a kissing noise into the receiver.

Caitlin couldn't contain herself any longer. She swung around just as Alec faced forward again. He returned the phone to the cradle, giving her a smile that was cool and a touch impersonal.

"Hi, how are you? I wasn't expecting to see you today."

"Who were you talking to?" she blurted, then blushed scarlet. "I'm sorry, it's none of my business, of course. Forget I asked that."

"Don't be embarrassed." He sounded kind, almost paternal. "I was talking to Jodie. We were making the final arrangements for our date tonight. We're going to the Lincoln Center Playhouse."

"Yes, so Dot told me. It seems everyone knew how well you and Jodie hit it off except me."

"You were busy. I didn't like to bother you with personal calls. Dot mentioned that you were up to your neck in paperwork."

"You've been talking to Dot? She never mentioned it."

"Dot and I have gotten to know each other quite well since Sam got sick. She and Betty seem to have become bosom buddies."

"Dot and Betty?" Caitlin exclaimed. "They like each other?"

"Why do you sound so surprised? They have a lot in common. Same age. Same profession. Both super-efficient. I understand they met for cocktails one evening and had a great time complaining about their respective bosses." Alec smiled blandly. "They seem to think we're doing a very bad job of managing our personal lives."

"They disapprove of your dating Jodie," Caitlin said quickly.

Alec's smile deepened. "On the contrary, they both think she's exactly the person I should be dating right now."

Caitlin found herself clutching her briefcase so hard her knuckles had turned white. She set the briefcase down and tried to achieve a casual smile. "I'm surprised you're having so much fun. I didn't expect you and Jodie to hit it off. There's, um ... there's kind of a big age gap between the two of you."

"Twelve, thirteen years is nothing these days. Jodie and I find we have the most amazing number of things in common. Attitudes to life, reactions to people, family values. All sorts of things."

Caitlin smothered a disbelieving snort. "Since when did you develop a fascination for the life cycle of the tsetse fly?"

"Gee, Jodie hasn't talked all that much about insects." Alec's mouth curved into a tender, reminiscent smile. "I guess we found more interesting ways to spend our time." He reached for a legal brief, then stopped in mid-motion, as if he'd just remembered Caitlin was in his office and he needed to mind his manners. "I'm sure you came here for a reason, Caity. A busy career person like you doesn't take time off in the middle of the afternoon just to shoot the breeze. Is there something I can help you with?"

So many things, she thought. *Dear God, so many things*.

Too late, she realized why Dot's news about Jodie had so upset her and why she had rushed to Alec's office: she had been fiercely, savagely jealous.

Things that had been opaque suddenly became crystal clear. Her flight across town had been the instinctive, reflexive action of a wild creature running from danger to the security of its lair.

Except that Alec was simultaneously both the safe lair, and the danger from which she was running.

How in the world had it taken her so long to recognize a truth so basic to her well-being, so fundamental to her life? For years now she had been fighting the knowledge that she loved Alec, that she desired him physically with a hunger that was fast becoming an incurable ache—and that she wanted to spend the rest of her days as his wife.

Putting the truth into words, even though she didn't speak them out loud, made her dizzy. Disoriented, she glanced vaguely around the office, wondering what she should do next in a world that had lost all its familiar bearings.

Alec got up quickly. For the first time that afternoon, he really seemed to see her, and he put his arm around her waist, guiding her to a chair. "What is it, Caity? You went white as a ghost." He spoke into the intercom. "Betty, could you please bring me some hot tea or coffee? And maybe a cracker or two? Whatever's available in the lunchroom."

His voice hardened when he turned back to speak to Caitlin. "You should take better care of yourself. Making yourself ill with overwork isn't going to be much help to Sam or anyone else."

"I'm not planning to work this weekend," Caitlin said. "For the next two days I'm on vacation."

"Good." He didn't suggest getting together with her over the weekend. He didn't mention their tentative plans for a visit to the zoo.

Betty came in with a pot of tea and a plate of small cookies. Looking at Caitlin, her frowns disappeared and her face softened into an expression of kindly sympathy. "My dear, you don't look well," she said. "Would a couple of aspirin help? It's all I've got to offer, I'm afraid."

Caitlin wished—fervently—that aspirin could cure what ailed her. Unfortunately lovesickness required more potent medicine. She forced herself to sit up straight and accept the cup of tea with a bright smile. She was darned if she'd betray weakness in front of the gorgon. "Thanks, Betty, but once I've had a leisurely dinner and a good night's sleep I'll be a new woman. This has been a busy week, that's all."

"Shall I call a cab for you?" Betty asked. "There might be a wait at this time on a Friday evening."

Alec spoke at once. "Don't bother with cabs, Betty, I'll take Caity home."

"You're forgetting your other appointment," Betty said, and her voice took on an odd sort of warning note. "You know you can't leave the office, Alec. Not now. Not with Ms. Howard."

"But, surely, in the circumstances..."

"I don't think it would be at all wise," Betty said firmly.

Alec walked over to the window and looked out into the gathering dusk, so Caitlin couldn't gauge his reaction to these instructions from his secretary. "Instructions" was the correct word, too, Caitlin thought, shocked at this further evidence of Betty's dislike. The secretary had come close to forbidding Alec to drive Caitlin home.

A few moments passed, and when Alec finally spoke, he continued to stare out of the window. "You're quite right, Betty. Thanks for reminding me. Caitlin and I will only be another few minutes and then I'll be ready for my next appointment."

"Good," she said. "I have all the papers on my desk. And I'll call Ms. Howard a cab."

Betty left the room and Alec turned away from the window, although he seemed to deliberately avoid meeting Caitlin's eye as he returned to his desk. Her hands started to shake, and she put down her cup to avoid spilling the dregs of her tea. It was an extraordinary feeling to look across the room at a man she had known for most of her life and realize that her knees wobbled and her heart pounded at the mere thought of his glancing up and meeting her gaze.

She wanted to run to his side, hurl herself into his arms and shout aloud how much she loved him, but a cruel voice deep inside her head whispered that if she did any such thing, she might well be humiliated. Twenty years of friendship linked their pasts, and yet she had no idea how Alec really felt about her. The cold truth was that she'd never allowed herself to consider his feelings. Her relationship with Alec had been dominated by *her* needs, *her* wishes, *her* desires. In a lifetime of friendship, she could remember few occasions when she'd inquired how Alec felt about a situation. She'd simply assumed—with blind arrogance—that he felt the same way she did. Their relationship was deeply rooted in the selfishness of her behavior, and she feared she would soon choke on the tangled weeds of her own creation.

Alec spoke at last. "Why did you come here this afternoon, Caity?"

She wanted to tell him. She searched for words that might begin to hint at the truths about herself she'd finally uncovered. Unfortunately she had no chance to speak. Betty displayed her unfailing knack for intruding at just the wrong moment and stuck her head around the door. "The cab will be here in ten minutes.

The dispatcher wants you to wait downstairs, Ms. Howard.''

Caitlin tried to sound properly grateful. "I'll be right down. Thanks for calling on my behalf.''

"Anytime." Betty withdrew.

Alec leaned forward across his desk. The rays of the setting sun angled through the window behind him, burnishing the sheen of his dark hair and outlining his high cheekbones in a vivid contrast of light and shadow. Caitlin's stomach swooped in a visceral response to the power of his sheer male sexuality. Had she been willfully blind these past few years? How had she managed to spend so much time with Alec and yet still cut off all awareness of her own feelings and her own physical attraction to him?

"Caity." Alec sounded gentle again, and yet remote. "You really don't look well. Take care of yourself this weekend, okay?''

"Sure." His impersonal kindness irritated her lacerated nerves more than any brusqueness could possibly have done. Until it stopped, she hadn't realized how much she cherished the undercurrent of husky, intimate warmth that always flowed beneath their conversations. Overwhelmed by a sudden need for the privacy of her own apartment, she got up and prepared to leave. She couldn't smile, so she pretended to busy herself picking up her briefcase and smoothing her skirt.

"Do you have plans for tonight?" Alec asked politely.

She tried to sound casual and unconcerned. "Very important ones. I plan to sleep for twelve hours and vegetate for another twelve after that."

Alec's gaze narrowed as he escorted her to the door. "You know, you still haven't told me why you came."

She bit back a gasp of slightly hysterical laughter. *For protection from the big bad wolf,* she thought. *Except you turned out to be the wolf, not the protector.*

"It was business," she said, clutching at the first excuse that popped into her overtired, overworked brain.

"Business? Oh, you must mean my contract with Services Unlimited. My search for a wife."

She hadn't meant that at all, of course. She could hardly think of anything she wanted to discuss less than Alec's quest for marital bliss. She sighed and rubbed her eyes, which burned with fatigue.

"I came to straighten out a possible misunderstanding," she said at last. "I want you to know I don't consider Jodie Bergen a client of our agency. She isn't on our books, and she wasn't introduced to you as a serious candidate for the position of your wife. As far as I'm concerned, anything that's developed between the two of you is strictly personal and has nothing to do with our company."

"Are you telling me I don't owe Services Unlimited any money?"

The question jarred and Caitlin gritted her teeth. "Naturally, since you and Jodie..." She cleared her throat and tried again. "In the circumstances, I'm willing to cancel your agreement with the company."

"You're jumping the gun a bit," Alec said. "I'm not sure I want you to do that."

They'd reached the door to his office and she stopped in surprise. "But you and Jodie—"

"Jodie is a great person, and we get on very well together, but marriage is a serious business. I'd certainly like to check out all my options before I take the final plunge."

Something wasn't right with this conversation, Caitlin thought, trying to prod her fuzzy brain cells into action. A few minutes ago, when she'd burst into his office, Alec had been calling Jodie "darling," and blowing kisses into the phone. Now he was talking about checking out the full range of his matrimonial options. The shift in his attitude made no sense, and Caitlin was about to say so. Second thoughts prompted her to keep silent. Heaven knew, after the way she'd behaved recently, she wasn't the right person to call other people's actions irrational.

"You were going to say something?" Alec prompted, ushering her out of his office.

Caitlin spoke in a low voice and hoped very much that Betty wasn't listening. "I just wondered... isn't it a little unfair to Jodie if you start dating other women?"

"Don't worry about Jodie—we understand each other much better than you'd expect," Alec said heartily. He gave a smooth smile and ushered her past Betty's desk toward the elevator. "Jodie's sweet, and I'm crazy about her already, but we both have a lot to consider before plunging into a lifetime commitment. So if you have a suitable bride on your books, I'd like to meet her. I trust your professional judgment, Caity, even if our old friendship is on rocky ground these days."

The wretched man was making absolutely no sense. Caitlin became aware of a complex new emotion, somewhere between excitement and anger, uncoiling in the pit of her stomach. "Let me get this straight," she said. "Despite the fact that you and Jodie are so attracted to each other that you spent every night this week together, you now want me to produce another candidate for the position of your wife?"

"That's right. And I'd appreciate a call from you every day or so tell me how your search is progressing. That way I can fill you in on my progress with Jodie, too." He made no effort to explain his motives or to defend his decision. She had the bizarre impression that, although they were discussing something that ought to have been of vital importance to him, his attention was elsewhere.

Caitlin abandoned her struggle to understand the incomprehensible. A thread of hope was added to her anger and her excitement. If Alec wasn't committed to Jodie, then Caitlin had been given another chance. Surely she could find some way to convince him that the perfect bride had been sitting under his nose for the past several years. She loved a challenge, and this was shaping up to be the most important one she'd ever tackled.

Caitlin found that she could smile again, and she flashed Alec one of her best professional smiles. "Okay, you've got a deal. As it happens, I have the perfect person in mind for you to date."

"You have?" He seemed startled, as well he might after her initial lack of enthusiasm for the assignment. "Well, er, great. What's her name?"

"Helen." Caitlin said the first name that popped into her head. "And that's all I'm telling you for now, Alec."

"When can I meet her?"

"Saturday evening."

"It's, um, rather short notice...."

"Take it or leave it, Alec. Helen's very much in demand. She has invitations for a party that the Mexican ambassador is hosting, and you could escort her. A genuine south-of-the-border fiesta, dancing, singing, good food and all the Washington bigwigs in attendance. Black tie. Eight o'clock. You can pick her up at my place. Interested?''

"I'll be there."

Caitlin's smile this time was entirely genuine. "Helen will be pleased,'' she said, and escaped into the elevator.

CHAPTER NINE

CAITLIN HAD ALWAYS considered herself smart, sensible and reasonably attractive. She could cope with most of life's intellectual challenges, although she wasn't an Einstein, or even a budding Ph.D like Jodie. She wasn't knockout gorgeous or gamin-cute like Michelle, but she had an acceptable face, perched on top of a decent body, with better-than-average legs and thick chestnut hair that was her secret pride and joy. Not bad qualities, all in all, even if she was so thickheaded about her own feelings that Alec had to be on the verge of marrying another woman before she noticed that she loved him.

By late Saturday afternoon, Caitlin was ready to revise her previous favorable opinion of herself. After hours of touring stores and trying on clothes, she reached the gloomy conclusion that she had seriously overestimated her physical attractions. On the evidence of the afternoon's shopping, she must be one of the ugliest, most misshapen women in the city of Washington. Nothing fit and she looked a fright in everything.

She'd given up hours ago on her dream of finding a dress so drop-dead stunning that Alec would take one look at her and realize what he'd been missing all his life. Now, she hoped for nothing fancier than a dress that would flatter her small waist and show off her legs, preferably in a color that didn't clash hopelessly with her hair. Hair that for some reason no longer appeared subtly chestnut, but seemed instead to glow more carroty orange with each outfit she tried on.

Smothering a sigh, Caitlin entered the small Georgetown boutique on Wisconsin Avenue that was her last stop before she gave up and went home. The Christmas merchandise was already in stock: rows of stiff dresses in heavy scarlet satin and black velvet; skirts and sweaters in winter white; and lots of blouses weighted down with sequins. None of it was even remotely like what she was looking for.

Without much hope, Caitlin turned from the new stock and poked through a rack of sale items, wondering why the capital of the United States of America was unable to provide such a simple commodity as one—just one—outfit capable of dazzling Alec Woodward.

When she first spotted the silk dress hidden among the bargains, she tried to damp down her flare of hope. But in the dressing room, staring at her reflection in the mirror, she couldn't restrain the quiver of pleasure that rippled down her spine.

The dress was everything she wanted. Of delicate green silk, shot through with a sheen of gold, the style was simple, with a close-fitting bodice, low neck and elbow-length sleeves. The skirt was gored and cut on the bias, so that its flare was subtle, starting below the hips and ending in soft swirls at the knee-length hem. Even without makeup and with her hair dragged back in a ponytail, the dress brought her closer to drop-dead stunning than she'd ever hoped to come. Surely Alec would take one look at her in this and forget all about Helen.

Which would be extremely fortunate, Caitlin reflected, owing to the fact that Helen didn't exist.

Her optimism lasted long enough to get her home, showered, zipped into the new dress and halfway through putting on her makeup. But somewhere between smoothing on lip gloss and stroking on mascara, doubt set in and she wondered if she was behaving like a total idiot.

Her plan had seemed quite straightforward yesterday, when it existed only inside her head: set up an interesting place to meet with Alec (the ambassador's Mexican fiesta); enjoy each other's company for a couple of hours (dance, eat tortillas, drink margaritas); then confess the truth about her feelings (Alec, I love you). The plan dissolved into vagueness at this point, but Caitlin had hoped it would include Alec sweeping her into his arms and setting a wedding date as they exchanged rapturous kisses.

Unfortunately, now that she was getting down to the nitty-gritty, her plan seemed to suffer from several gaping holes. Alec was too polite to refuse to go out with her when she failed to produce the nonexistent Helen, but that was no guarantee the evening would be a success, or even a semi-success. If their encounter yesterday was anything to judge by, tonight could well be an unmitigated disaster.

Poking hairpins into a sophisticated, upswept hairstyle that refused to stay either upswept or sophisticated, Caitlin discovered the awkward truth that the more intense your feelings, the more difficult they were to put into words.

I love you. How could it possibly be difficult to say three such simple words to a man she had known most of her life?

She clipped on earrings that shimmered against her cheeks in a fragile burst of golden moons and crystal stars. The earrings had been a gift from Alec last Christmas, and Caitlin suddenly felt more cheerful. So what if she now realized she loved Alec Woodward? How could she possibly feel nervous about a date with him? Heck, the first time they met, he'd still been wearing braces and she was a third-grader with scabby knees.

Since leaving college, she'd slept on his sofa plenty of times and spent dozens of weekends in his company. She knew which part of the newspaper he read first on Sundays. He'd seen her looking hot and frazzled after mowing her parents' lawn, and she knew what he looked like before he drank that crucial first cup of coffee in the morning. Good grief, what was she worried about? They might as well be married already, they knew each other so intimately.

Her doorbell rang and her hand stopped in midair. Alec. It had to be Alec, otherwise the night watchman would have buzzed the intercom to alert her to visitors. Caitlin's stomach swooped as she stuck a final pin into her hair and left the bathroom. Her high heels sounded extraordinarily loud as she crossed the parquet floor of the tiny entrance hall. Tap, tap, tap. Her heartbeat echoed her heels, only twice as fast. Pitpat, pitpat, pitpat. She pushed at a wisp of hair that had already lost its moorings and drew a shaky breath. This was it! *Showtime.*

She threw open the door, smiling a cheery welcome. No point in making a mountain out of a molehill, she chided herself. Keep calm, think cool, and this won't be so bad.

It wasn't going to be bad, it was going to be terrible, far worse than her worst nightmare, she knew the moment she saw him. Immaculate in evening dress and starched white shirt, Alec stood on her doorstep, holding a small gift-wrapped box. He looked inches taller than she remembered him, a hundred times more suave and about a thousand times more sexy. His blue eyes swept her appraisingly, and for a split second, she saw the leap of some primitive emotion blaze in the depths of his gaze. Then the fire was banked, and he smiled at her with remote courtesy.

"Hello, Caity. You're all dressed up. Going somewhere exciting?"

She had to say something, invent some excuse, or the evening would be over before it got started. "Come in, Alec, would you?" Her voice sounded high and squeaky, about as sophisticated as Minnie Mouse, and she coughed nervously.

"I'm afraid things, um ... things aren't quite going to plan." Heaven knew, that was certainly true.

Alec strolled in and tossed his white silk scarf over the back of a chair. Men like Alec should be banned from wearing evening dress, Caitlin thought wildly. It wasn't fair to the female half of the population. How could she think when her entire body had transformed itself into a quivering collection of hormones?

"Where's Helen?" he asked, glancing around the empty living room. "I'm looking forward to meeting her and finding out how much we have in common."

Caitlin hoped she didn't look as guilty as she felt. "Um ... there's a slight problem," she said. "I'm really sorry, but, um, Helen's been called away at the last minute. Urgent. A very urgent matter."

Alec looked startled. "Called away? That is a surprise. Nothing tragic has happened, I hope."

Caitlin sensed events slipping disastrously out of her control. By now she should have confessed to Alec that Helen didn't exist and they should both be laughing at the joke. But the simple words of explanation wouldn't come. Alec wasn't looking at her, he wasn't laughing with her, he scarcely seemed aware of her existence. At this precise moment, Caitlin would have preferred to enter the cage of a dozen starving leopards than confess the truth about Helen to Alec.

"It was a top-level meeting. International business. The people are only in town for one night," she said quickly. "Just one of those last-minute crises Helen is always coping with. She asked me to give you her sincere apologies. I'm afraid it may be a while before she's available again."

"I'm devastated. I was really looking forward to meeting her. What does she do precisely?"

"Do?"

"Yes, you know, what's her profession? Where does she work?"

"For the government," Caitlin said after a too-long pause. "Very hush-hush. Top-level security clearance. I really shouldn't say anything more."

"I'm flattered she wants to take time out from such an exciting job to meet me."

"Well, I've told her a lot about you."

He chuckled. "Then I'm even more surprised she wants to meet me. How did she come to be a client of yours?"

"She needed reliable cleaning help."

"And you managed to talk her into considering marriage to me? Wow! I always knew you were a good salesperson, but not that good. What color hair does she have?"

"Red." Caitlin said the first thing that came into her head.

"Like yours? What a coincidence."

"No, it's not a coincidence. She's nothing at all like me. She's more of a strawberry blonde."

"Mmm. Sounds delightful."

Caitlin tried to think of some witty comeback and failed totally. In fact, she couldn't think of anything to say at all. Alec broke the silence.

"Well, I can see you're ready to leave for somewhere fancy. I guess I'd better head for home."

"You could come with me," Caitlin blurted out. *Good Lord, what a mess she was making of this simple invitation!*

Alec picked up his scarf. "Oh, no, I wouldn't want to intrude on a special date."

"Don't worry, it's not a special date. I don't have a date. I got dressed up for you." She blushed hotly. "What I mean is Helen sent over her invitation cards for the Mexican fiesta and asked me to take you in her place."

He looked doubtful in the extreme. "But we don't want to go to a party together, do we? What's the point? We'd both be more usefully employed catching up on our paperwork."

"I'm not working this weekend, remember?"

"Then you certainly don't have to fill in for Helen, Caity. Relax and enjoy your mini-vacation. I quite understand why your client couldn't make it."

He was turning the doorknob, on the brink of leaving. Caitlin couldn't believe how badly she'd handled the situation. "I don't want to catch up on paperwork," she said flatly. "I really would like to go to this fiesta with you, Alec. If you feel you can spare the time, that is. I don't want to impose."

Alec opened the door. "I'm sorry, I really can't..." He paused, then slowly swung around. She had the odd impression that he was annoyed with himself for staying. "All right," he said curtly. "Since we're both dressed up already, it seems a bit silly to end the evening before it's even started."

"Oh, yes!" she agreed fervently. "We may as well go to the embassy and strut our stuff. It should be fun."

"If you say so." Alec leaned against the doorjamb, finally looking at her with eyes that actually seemed to focus. "I like your dress. Have I ever seen it before?"

"No, it's new." She tried not to feel crushed, but she'd hoped for so much more from this glamorous outfit than an offhand compliment. She was darn sure he would remember which dresses he'd seen Jodie wear and which ones were new. She forced a smile, drawing some comfort from the fact that her plans for the evening could still be salvaged. At least he hadn't refused outright to take her to the party. At least he was willing to spend a few hours in her company.

"You need a coat," he said. "It's chilly out there tonight."

"Right. If you'll wait a second, I'll get it."

He smothered a yawn that appeared bored rather than tired. "Take your time. No reason to rush."

THE PARTY WAS in full swing by the time Caitlin and Alec arrived. Waiters circulated through the reception rooms carrying heavy silver trays laden with chilled champagne and foaming margaritas. Crowds of elegantly clothed men and women clustered around buffet tables that were almost invisible beneath bowls and platters of spicy seafood, fajitas, tacos, salsas, salads, salty breadsticks and colorful tropical fruits. Strolling musicians entertained the guests with folk songs, and in a vaulted room with two magnificently tiled alcoves, a larger band played traditional Mexican dance music for the few couples who seemed interested in dancing.

Caitlin was glad of the noise and the bustle of activity, since she and Alec seemed to have absolutely nothing to say to each other. Poised awkwardly near the end of one of the buffet tables, they nibbled food that Caitlin suspected neither of them wanted and exchanged polite platitudes about nothing in particular.

Alec finally suggested they should go to the room with the dancing, but the band had chosen that moment to take a break, and they were left with nothing to do except prop up one of the walls and sip margaritas. When Caitlin saw a diplomat who had been a client of Services Unlimited earlier in the year, she greeted him eagerly.

"Antonio, I'm so glad to see you. How are you?"

He bowed gracefully over her hand. Despite years at graduate school in the States and several more years in Washington, he hadn't lost any of his Latin charm. "All the better for seeing you, Caitlin. I keep meaning to fire my housekeeper so I have an excuse to call you and arrange a long, intimate lunch."

She laughed. "You don't need such a drastic excuse—just call. I'd love to have lunch with you. Although I'd be delighted to find you a new housekeeper if you really need one."

"Serafina keeps talking about retiring. Joking aside, I may have to contact you soon." His gaze roamed approvingly over her legs and lingered on the bare slope of her shoulders. "That's a terrific dress you have on, Caitlin, just the right color for you. And your hair looks more gorgeous than usual."

She smiled. "Thanks. I see you still manage to say all the things a woman wants to hear."

"With you, it's easy because they're all true." He held out his hand to Alec. "We haven't met, but I recognize you from the evening news on television. I am Antonio de las Canteras, information officer at the Mexican Embassy, and you are Alec Woodward, famous defense lawyer for the notorious Mr. Mancuso."

Alec grimaced as he shook hands. "Right now, I wish Mr. Mancuso were a little less well-known, and I wish the press hadn't decided to make his wife into their victim-of-the-month. The finer points of law tend to get lost when a trial is carried on in the full blaze of media attention."

"But you are well accustomed to such trials, no? You are famous for keeping cool under pressure."

Alec gave a tight smile. "If that's a compliment, I guess I'd better grab it and say thank-you."

"It was most certainly a compliment." Antonio broke off, cocking his head to one side. He smiled in delight. "Listen, the band is playing a tango—how fortunate for me. Caitlin, I'm going to beg and plead and make a pest of myself until you agree to dance with me. I have vivid memories of the last time we performed a tango together, and I'm going to claim the privilege of a host and insist on repeating the pleasure."

Caitlin was more than willing to accept. Not only was Antonio a superb dancer, but the tension between Alec and her seemed to be building by the minute, and she was frankly relieved at the prospect of spending some time away from him. She murmured a few conventional words to excuse herself and gladly followed Antonio onto the dance floor.

Handsome, slender and athletic, Antonio harbored no Anglo-Saxon hang-ups about modesty or not making a spectacle of himself. He knew from previous encounters that Caitlin loved to dance, and he quickly led her into a series of dramatic twirls, followed by a couple of even more dramatic lunges with her back arched over his supporting arm and her skirt swirling about his knees in a flash of golden-green silk. An appreciative audience gathered around the edge of the dance floor, and Caitlin allowed herself to strut, glide and swoop in response to Antonio's expert commands. The harder she threw herself into her performance, the easier it was to forget about Alec and the disaster this evening had become. Exerting every ounce of her technical skill, she did her best to lose herself in the pounding, exotic rhythm of the dance. When the music finally ended and the crowd applauded, she emerged blinking and disoriented into reality. A quick glance around revealed that Alec had left the room. Obviously he found her company so boring he hadn't bothered to stay and watch.

Antonio mopped his brow with a snow-white handkerchief, seized two champagne flutes from a passing waiter and handed her one. He raised his glass in a toast. "You get better every time, Caitlin."

"Thanks. So do you." She drank deeply, vaguely remembering that she'd already had two margaritas but too thirsty to care. She wondered where Alec had gone and wished he had been her partner for the tango. Dancing with Antonio was fun, but dancing with Alec was heaven.

"We seem to have lost your escort," Antonio murmured. "What a stroke of good fortune for me. I shall start my grand plan to seduce you immediately. Caitlin, you have the most adorable green eyes and a mouth that is so kissable I'm already driven insane with longing. Get rid of your uptight lawyer and come home with me tonight."

Caitlin laughed. "Don't say that with such a soulful sigh, Antonio, or some unsuspecting woman might believe you were serious."

He tucked her hand through his arm. "I am serious—why do you doubt me? I would like nothing better than to take you to my bed tonight."

"On condition that I promise to leave before dawn tomorrow morning, right?"

He grinned. "For you, beautiful Caitlin, I would make an exception. You can stay until ten o'clock and help yourself to coffee and freshly squeezed orange juice before you leave."

"What a deal! I'm truly flattered, but I guess I'll pass all the same."

He sighed. "I knew I had no hope when I saw your glowering lawyer. He's tough competition even for a man like me."

"He's not *my* lawyer," Caitlin said, then wished she hadn't spoken when Antonio looked at her with too much understanding.

"You sound frustrated, *pequeña.*"

"You're mistaken. Alec and I have known each other for years, but we're just good friends."

"Ah!" he said. "I see."

"There's nothing to see."

"But of course there is. You wish him to be something more than a friend, and he is not cooperating.

Although why he refuses to cooperate I can't imagine. The mating behavior of you Americanos is often incomprehensible to the Latin soul.''

Caitlin swallowed the last mouthful of her champagne. The bubbles fizzed in her throat and she suddenly felt reckless enough to admit the truth. "You're right about one thing, Antonio. I want him to be a lot more than my friend."

"Then tell him so. Better yet, show him."

"I tried. He isn't getting the message."

"You are too subtle in affairs of the heart. Don't beat around the bush. Don't drop delicate hints. Take him home to your apartment and make love to him until he's too tired to keep his feelings hidden behind those defensive shields he carries. I can't imagine any way for a woman to be more convincing than in her lover's bed."

Caitlin wasn't sure whether to laugh or cry. "Antonio, you make it sound a snap. But somehow I don't think it's quite that easy to turn an old friend into a lover."

"If you're willing to risk the friendship, it's easy. In your case, trust me. You have only to kiss your uptight, controlled lawyer with passion, to look at him with hunger in your eyes, to allow your body to show your needs, and I guarantee you will be in his bed as fast as he can get you there. Alec Woodward wants to make love to you, Caitlin, take my word for it. Desire is not something one man can hide from another, not even your oh-so-controlled lawyer."

She traced the rim of her empty glass with her fingertip. "Maybe he does want to make love to me," she said. "But physical attraction isn't enough. What happens if our lovemaking doesn't work out? I'd hate to ruin a great friendship with Alec for the sake of an unsuccessful one-night stand.''

He shrugged. "Life is full of risks, Caitlin. You have merely to decide if winning the game is worth the stake you're investing."

She smiled ruefully. "I don't believe life's equations are as simple as you're making them sound, Antonio."

His answering smile didn't quite reach his eyes. "A cynic always finds other people's romantic problems easy to resolve. It is his own love affairs that he manages so badly." He gave her no chance to probe this brief glimpse beneath his facade.

"Look!" he said, all suave charm once again. "There is your heartthrob lawyer. He seems to have a harem of devoted admirers in tow."

"He usually does at parties like this."

"Then we must break him loose." Taking Caitlin's hand, Antonio drew her across the room and ended up in front of Alec, pushing her forward with a flourish.

"Mr. Woodward, I thank you from the bottom of my heart for allowing me to dance with Caitlin. She tangos with such fire and grace that it's always thrilling to be her partner."

"There's no reason to thank me," Alec said curtly. "Caitlin doesn't need my permission to choose a dance partner."

"How generous of you," Antonio murmured. "For myself, with such a beautiful woman as my date, I believe I would be a little more possessive." He took Caitlin's hand, dropped a kiss onto her fingertips and slipped away into the crowd without saying another word.

Alec disengaged himself from the cluster of women surrounding him. "This has been a terrific party and it's been great talking to you all. I appreciate your good wishes for Mr. Mancuso, and I'll be sure to pass them on to him. Caitlin, are you ready to leave now?''

She drew in a deep breath, wishing they weren't being overheard by so many people. "Are we in a hurry?" she asked. "I'd love to dance with you before we leave."

For a moment, she thought he was going to refuse. Then he shrugged and put his hand on the small of her back, guiding her to the dance floor without speaking. For once, luck seemed to be on her side. As Alec took her into his arms, the band finished an energetic mamba and segued into the compelling, melancholy rhythms of a folk song lamenting the heartache caused by a false lover.

As Alec drew her fractionally closer, Caitlin realized she was shaking. The longing to lean against him, to mold her softness against the hardness of his body, was intense enough to make her feel dizzy. Or perhaps the dizziness was caused by two margaritas and a tall glass of champagne. Or perhaps this was how people always felt when they were falling in love. She'd never understood before how accurate the word "falling" actually was. She felt disoriented, giddy, dazzled, by the intensity of her emotions.

Alec's hand rested lightly, noncommittally against the small of her back as he guided her across the dance floor. The lightness of his touch drove her crazy. She wanted to feel his fingers clutch her with urgent need. She wanted him to drag her tight against him and drown her yearnings in a sea of endless, stormy passion.

Alec, however, might as well have been dancing with the Queen of England for all the passion he displayed. In fact, if he'd been dancing with the Queen, he'd have felt compelled to make polite conversation, which was a lot more than he was attempting right now. Frustration began to spice Caitlin's longing with a dash of desperation, and with a boldness that would have been unimaginable a couple of weeks earlier, she closed the six-inch gap between their bodies and allowed her hands to caress his back with erotic, feathery strokes. Emboldened by the shudder of his response, she clasped her fingers behind his neck and pulled his cheek down to rest against hers.

The smell of his after-shave filled her nostrils; the heat of his body warmed her soul. Desire and happiness bubbled through her veins. She wondered how she could have deprived herself of these incredible feelings for so many years. How could she have fooled herself into thinking she wanted Alec as a friend, when her entire being craved him as a lover? As a husband... The lights dimmed and she closed her eyes, rubbing her face softly against his.

His reaction was all she'd hoped for. He stumbled and for several seconds couldn't recapture the beat of the music. As soon as their steps were in sync again, he led her to the darkest corner of the dance floor, and she felt his clasp tighten around her, cradling her hips against his lower body, showing her how much he desired her. His hands no longer felt cool and remote, but hot and urgent, just as she'd longed for. Then he bent his head and for a few blissful moments she felt the brush of his hungry kisses in the hollow of her neck. Her skin tingled, her body pulsed with desire. Oblivious to their surroundings, she turned her head, lifting her face to receive the full-blown kiss she craved.

For an instant, his mouth hovered over hers. She saw his eyes darken with passion until they were almost indigo; she saw the tension in the tight line of his jaw and knew he wanted to kiss her as desperately as she wanted to receive his kiss. Then he snapped his head up, jerking away from her. And when he faced her again, his expression had completely changed.

"Tell me more about Helen," he said, as if two seconds earlier he hadn't been poised on the brink of kissing her senseless. "I'm really longing to hear all about her. Adventurous, dynamic, sure of herself—she sounds just my type."

Caitlin felt like Alice in Wonderland at the Mad Hatter's tea party. Why were they suddenly talking about Helen? Why was Alec guiding her with such determination toward the well-lit center of the room? She blinked, trying to slough the haze of desire that clung to her like a second skin. She couldn't think of anything she wanted to discuss less than the wretched, nonexistent Helen. She shook her head, frantically trying to collect her muzzy thoughts.

"Are you feeling all right?" Alec asked kindly. "We can sit out the rest of this dance if you prefer."

"Yes, that would be better. I think that last glass of champagne did me in."

Alec looked at his watch. "Actually, it's already eleven-thirty. Why don't we slip away before it gets really late? I'm sure you have as much to do tomorrow as I do, so we could both use an early night."

Caitlin stared at him in helpless silence, which he read as consent. As he ushered her briskly toward the exit, she had the bewildering sensation that somewhere between one blink of her eyes and the next, an alien had slipped into Alec's body and taken possession. It wasn't possible for the man who had trembled in her arms to sound this casual and cheery two minutes later.

"Alec...about Helen...about us..."

His smile never waivered. "Look, Caitlin, you don't have to explain. There is no *us*. I understand completely."

"What happened on the dance floor..."

"I apologize," he said with a disarming shrug. "What can I say? I'm a sucker for slow music. It has a crazy effect on my libido, but don't worry, Caity, I promise you it didn't mean a thing." He rushed on before she could say a word. "You know, I've been thinking about Helen. I'm not sure you should arrange a meeting between the two of us, after all. The more I think about it, the more I wonder how we'd make a marriage work. My schedule's impossible, and hers sounds as if it's even worse. Besides, Jodie is the ideal candidate. She hasn't established her career as yet, so her life-style is more flexible. We'll be able to accommodate each other's needs much more easily. It seems superfluous to bring another woman into the picture at this stage."

"That's fine with me," Caitlin said. "Helen is history." She was so grateful to be let off the hook that she didn't risk pointing out that it had been entirely Alec's own idea to meet another candidate. If she hadn't felt so heartsick and bemused, she would have spared a few moments to inform Alec that he was behaving like a potential chauvinist, and that Jodie deserved more out of life than to be picked as a wife simply because she was young and not yet settled into a career.

Alec retrieved their coats from the cloakroom and helped Caitlin into hers with polite solicitude. "We'll consider the Helen situation settled, then."

"Fine, terrific. Helen never existed." She blushed hotly. "As far as you're concerned, I mean."

"Right, as far as I'm concerned, she was just a figment of your imagination." Alec whistled cheerfully, jingling the coins in his pocket as they waited for a parking attendant to bring them their car. "Well, I guess there's nothing left to say except here's to dear little Jodie, and congratulations to you, Caity, on your terrific matchmaking skills. Thanks to you, Jodie and I are making the perfect team!"

"Rah-rah," Caitlin said, horrified to discover she was choking back tears. The enormity of her loss almost overwhelmed her. Because of her emotional immaturity and her panicky refusal to see that marriage to Alec would bear no resemblance to her parents' constricting relationship, she'd thrown away her chance to marry the man she'd been in love with since her sixteenth birthday.

"I'm seeing Jodie tomorrow," Alec said, opening the car door for her and tipping the attendant at the same time. "I've decided we should start making serious plans for a wedding. We'll have to talk about setting the date." He smiled widely. "My mother's going to be so excited—she's been planning my wedding for years."

"She and Sam will both be pleased," Caitlin managed to say. "And your father, of course."

Alec chuckled. "Sam will be tickled pink. This is all his idea. With a little help from Dot and Betty."

"Betty! What's she got to do with it?"

"Betty's been on a campaign to get me married. She's a real sentimentalist at heart." He latched his seat belt, looking so darn pleased with himself that Caitlin had an almost irresistible urge to bop him on the nose. Beneath her hurt, beneath her aching sense of loss, she felt bewildered. Lord knew, her behavior tonight hadn't been very rational, but Alec's had been even less rational. She had the crazy impression he was laughing at some joke she didn't share.

"I'm going to go straight home and telephone Jodie," he announced, easing the car out into the flow of traffic.

"You're going to ask her to set a date for your wedding?"

"Not exactly." Alec's face split into another wide grin. "My mother's had the date of my wedding picked out for at least a month," he said. "I just need to make sure that Jodie and Sam can clear their calendars for the first Saturday in December."

"December fifth?"

"Right."

In less than six weeks, Alec would be married. To Jodie. "Congratulations," Caitlin said, and even to her own ears, her voice sounded hollow. "I hope you'll both be very happy."

CHAPTER TEN

"HE CAN'T DO IT!" Caitlin said, pacing the hearth rug in Dot's cozy apartment. "We have to get him declared temporarily insane, or something. Good grief, Dot, can you imagine how miserable they're going to make each other?"

"Jodie's a nice kid. She'll make a great wife some day."

"*Some day*—that's the whole point. Five years from now when she's got the tsetse flies out of her system. But right now, she's not ready to be married, especially to a dynamic, demanding man like Alec. He's such a powerful personality he'll chew her up into little pieces. And while Jodie's trying to work out how to put herself together again, he'll decide she's boring and demand a divorce."

"Sounds like typical male behavior," Dot agreed.

"Alec isn't callous, not in the least. But I know him better than anyone, his faults as well as his good points. He needs a strong partner to stand up to him, not a kitten still trying to decide what she'll be when she finally grows up and has a full set of claws."

Dot yawned. "You sound very passionate about all this, boss, and I can't imagine why. Maybe Jodie's smarter than you think. Maybe she'll refuse to set a date for their wedding."

"Women never refuse Alec Woodward," Caitlin said gloomily. "Besides, she thinks she's in love with him. Everyone agrees on that."

"Have you actually talked to Jodie herself about how she feels?"

"Well, no...,"

"Then until you do, I suggest this conversation is premature. You know how I feel about marriage, it's not a subject I enjoy discussing, particularly on a Sunday morning before I've finished reading the newspaper. Have another blueberry muffin and let's talk about something else. Something more cheerful than marriage. How about income tax returns, or the Second World War?"

"I'm not hungry, thanks." Caitlin rubbed her forehead which had been throbbing with pain ever since she'd woken up that morning, a fitting punishment for too many margaritas and too little self-control. "Honestly, I think Alec has flipped. His behavior last night made absolutely no sense. One minute he was just about ready to make love to me right there on the dance floor—" She stopped abruptly. "I need another cup of coffee. Can I get you something?"

"A dash of honesty would be nice," Dot said.

Caitlin straightened, full of righteous indignation. "What does that mean, for heaven's sake? I came here this morning because you're a friend and I need your help—"

"And so far, you've consumed three large mugs of coffee and spouted on about everything except what's really worrying you."

"Which is?" Caitlin asked, very much on her dignity.

"The fact that you're head over heels in love with Alec Woodward."

Caitlin opened her mouth to protest, then collapsed onto the sofa in a defeated heap. "Oh, boy, is it that obvious?"

"Well, I guess a deaf and blind visitor from another planet might not get the picture." Dot shot her a shrewd glance. "Alec Woodward might not get the picture, either, since he appears to be as thick-skulled as you, impossible as that might seem. All in all, I'd say the two of you make an ideal couple. There can't be many people around with sky-high IQs and such a total lack of common sense."

Caitlin stared at her hands. "Alec's known me for years. If he wants to marry me, why hasn't he ever suggested it?"

"Would you have said yes? Or would you have gone running a thousand miles in the opposite direction? Face it, lady, you've never made any secret of the fact that, until recently, you considered marriage barely one step up from a sentence of life imprisonment."

Caitlin wasn't prepared to concede the logic of Dot's argument. "If Alec had wanted to marry me, he'd have said something by now. He must have recognized how I feel about him."

"I'd say that's highly debatable."

"He's just trying to save my pride by refusing to give me any chance to discuss my feelings. He's doing his best to stop me from telling him I love him."

"Honey, if you weren't so smart, I'd say you were terminally stupid."

"What's that supposed to mean?"

"Hasn't it occurred to you that Alec may find it as difficult to be honest with you as you are with him?"

"No, it hasn't," Caitlin said slowly. "The fact is, I have trouble seeing this situation from Alec's point of view. I keep trying to consider his emotions, his feelings, but my own needs get in the way. Right now, all I can think about is how much I want to be with him, how desperately I want him to hold me." She got up and renewed her pacing. "This falling-in-love business is totally weird, you know, and I don't have any practice in coping. My sisters would have known years ago how they felt. Good grief, they'd probably have known from the day Alec moved in next door that they planned to marry him. Whereas dumb old me, I only noticed last week that I'm madly, passionately in love with the wretched man."

"Madly?" Dot queried with obvious interest. "Passionately?" She smiled. "Well, boss, I guess that red hair of yours is coming into its own at last."

"And a lot of good it's doing me," Caitlin said tartly. "For heaven's sake, Dot, Alec and I are both adults. We're good friends. Why can't I just walk up to him and say, 'Alec, I love you. Would you be interested in spending the rest of your life with me?'"

Dot's laughter held a hint of pain. "Honey, I've been married three times, widowed once and divorced twice. If I knew the answer to that question I'd have written a how-to-manage-your-love-life book and made myself a fortune long before now. And I wouldn't have two divorces on my record. If you're looking for advice, you've come to the wrong woman."

"Maybe I should go over to his apartment tonight. Maybe I should go right now, before he meets with Jodie again." Caitlin squared her shoulders, mentally preparing herself for the task of confronting Alec. She looked at Dot and gave a gasp of embarrassed laughter. "You know, I really am going crazy. I've turned up on Alec's doorstep uninvited at least a hundred times. Suddenly, just because I've discovered I'm desperately in love with him, I can't do it."

"Love sure makes fools out of all of us," Dot agreed.

Something about Dot's tone penetrated the haze of Caitlin's self-absorption. "Dot, are you okay?" she asked. She looked more closely at her friend and saw that her eyes were suspiciously red-rimmed and her normally pink cheeks pale and sallow. Furious with herself for being so self-centered she had taken this long to notice that something was wrong, she knelt beside Dot's chair and took her hand. "Dot, what is it? Please tell me if I can help."

Dot stared at her empty coffee mug and the color came and went in her cheeks. Caitlin felt her heart constrict when Dot—the ever cheerful, ever cynical, ever self-possessed Dot—burst into noisy, wrenching tears.

Caitlin put her arm around Dot's shoulder and hugged her hard. "It'll be all right," she said soothingly. "Dot, tell me. Let me help. What is it?"

Dot's voice throbbed with tragedy. "I told Sam I'll marry him," she said. "Last night at nine o'clock. I promised him again this morning."

"*You told Sam you'll marry him!*" Caitlin repeated in a dazed voice. She rocked back on her heels, trying to absorb the stunning news. Keeping her arm around Dot, she probed the cause of her friend's tears as tactfully as she could. "You agreed because he's sick, is that what you mean? He wants to marry you, and you felt you couldn't refuse because he's suffered two minor heart attacks?"

Dot jerked out of Caitlin's comforting hug and stormed angrily across the room. "Of course not!" she said. "Sam's a wonderful, wonderful man and I've loved him for months. Oh, hell, where are the tissues?"

"Here."

Dot scrubbed her eyes and blew her nose. "I love Sam," she said harshly. "He's been asking me to marry him for weeks now, but I kept putting him off, telling him to find another woman."

"Why would you do that?" Caitlin asked cautiously. She was no expert in matters of the heart, but since Dot loved Sam and he loved her, she couldn't begin to understand why a proposal of marriage should have Dot hovering on the verge of hysterics.

Dot didn't answer directly. "We've been dating each other on and off since our Fourth of July office party. Of course, I've tried to make it more off than on, but Sam won't take no for an answer."

"That's good, isn't it? Doesn't that show how much he cares for you?"

Dot gave her a withering look. "After everyone else left the office party, we went to the beach and dug for clams. Then we sat up all night on the porch of his beach cottage just talking." The memory of this sentimental occasion was apparently enough to send her off into a fresh noisy bout of tears.

Caitlin stared at her secretary and wondered if "love" was simply another word for insanity. So far, Dot's story had revealed absolutely no reason for sadness. Dot, clearly, was in love with Sam. Sam, presumably, was in love with Dot, since he'd asked her to marry him. Sam's health, provided he followed a sensible diet and exercise regimen, was unlikely to present further problems. Dot was healthy as a horse. They were both single and free to marry. Caitlin tried to think of any possible reason her secretary would announce the news of her engagement as if it were the greatest disaster since the sinking of the *Titanic*. Absolutely no rational explanation came to mind.

"Does Sam want a long engagement?" she asked with what she hoped was supreme tact.

She had, apparently, blundered straight to the heart of an emotional mine field. "He wants to get married next Saturday!" Dot wailed. "In his house, with all the children there, and his friend the judge to conduct the ceremony, and he's already booked the Grand Gourmet catering service to prepare the buffet for afterward."

"It sounds as if he has everything well planned," Caitlin said. "The Grand Gourmet people are very good." She waited nervously and saw with relief that she'd finally managed to say something that didn't send Dot off into paroxysms of tears. She plucked up her courage and tried again. "I could help you choose a dress," she suggested. "You'd look wonderful in deep rose, or even burgundy, which would be a great color for this time of year."

Dot huddled on the edge of an armchair, shredding tissues. "I can't marry him," she said tersely. "I'll ruin his life. Look at me, for heaven's sake! Forty-five years old, and three marriages already behind me. Face it, Caitlin, I'm a loser where marriage is concerned, a lousy three-time loser."

"You're scared," Caitlin said. "Too scared to carry through on the commitment you've made to Sam."

"Darn right I'm scared. I have reason to be. Sam's a good man, a kind, generous man, who spent thirty years happily married to the same woman until he was widowed. He doesn't know what hell an unsuccessful marriage can be."

"On the other hand, you don't know what heaven a successful marriage can be," Caitlin pointed out. "Your first husband died in Vietnam before you were nineteen, and your other two marriages ended in divorce."

"Not entirely because my husbands were rats. Face it, Caitlin, I'm not easy to live with. I can be ornery as a hungry bear for no good reason and—"

"Whereas Sam is the model of sweet reason," Caitlin said, suddenly finding the situation almost amusing. "Five-thirty on Friday afternoons is just another example of his calm, cheerful approach to life. Come on, Dot, lighten up. In my opinion, the pair of you are two ornery bears who are going to make each other very happy."

"Do you really think that?" Dot sounded nothing at all like her usual confident, hard-edged self.

"Yes, I do," Caitlin said, and realized she was telling the absolute and complete truth.

"I get sick with nerves just thinking about telling his kids what we're planning," Dot said. "I'm supposed to go over to Sam's house for lunch today and face the music. Will you come with me?"

"Well, if you're sure it's not strictly a family occasion..."

"I need you." Dot managed a near-normal grin. "Having you around is living proof that everyone behaves like a total fool when they fall in love."

Reminded of her own crazy situation, Caitlin hesitated. "Alec won't be there with Jodie, will he? He said something about having a date with her today."

"It must be for the afternoon," Dot said. "Sam set up this lunch with Jodie and Laura, his other daughter. His son's going to be there, too. He flies back to

Chicago this evening. Please come, Caitlin. I need someone there who's on my side."

DOT COULDN'T HAVE BEEN more wrong in expecting to meet opposition from Sam's family. His children greeted the news of their father's impending marriage with crows of delight and fervent words of thanks to Dot for agreeing to take Sam in hand. They agreed with Caitlin that Dot would look wonderful in a wedding gown of deep rose and suggested that Caitlin would make a spectacular maid of honor in forest green. Laura confessed to being a whiz with a sewing maching, and Dot finally conceded that she *might* go out with Laura on Monday and choose the necessary dress patterns.

Sam, silver hairs spiking in a quiver of pleasure, sat on the sofa with his arm around Dot, looking as smug and self-satisfied as if he'd personally invented the concept of matrimony. His only complaint centered on Dot's insistence that he should toast their engagement with a glass of cranberry juice.

"Don't make a fuss," Dot said briskly. "I need you fighting fit for next Saturday."

"Ah, yes, the honeymoon," Sam said, looking extremely pleased with himself. "We're going to the Cayman Islands for a few days. Can you hold the fort at the office until I get back, Caitlin?"

"Covering for you will be a breeze, but I've no idea how I'll manage without Dot," she said, smiling. "But I'll try to keep everything together."

A ring of the doorbell interrupted a chorus of laughter from Sam's children. Jodie jumped up. "That must be Alec," she said. "I arranged to meet him here right around this time. I'll let him in."

Caitlin's laughter died abruptly. Conversation and jokes continued to ebb and flow around her, but she no longer heard them. She strained her ears and heard the sound of Jodie's voice raised in greeting and the low, husky murmur of Alec's response. They seemed to have an awful lot to say to each other out there in the privacy of the hallway, and at least ten minutes went by before Alec followed Jodie into the living room. He went straight to Sam and offered his hearty congratulations. Then he hugged Dot and told her she was a brave woman. Caitlin's presence he acknowledged with no more than a brief nod.

She watched him in the sort of rapt silence she'd always considered totally absurd in other people. The quirk of his mouth when he smiled, the restless energy of his body, the thickness of his hair all seemed new to her, and yet oddly familiar, as if they had always been part of her unconscious definition of masculinity. Last night, when he had worn evening dress, she had told herself it was the formal clothing that gave him such a compelling aura of magnetism. Today he was dressed in washed-out jeans and a loose-fitting, dark blue sweater, and he still dominated the room by his mere presence. Drinking in the reality of his nearness, it was all Caitlin could do to stay in her seat and not run to his side and beg for a few crumbs of his attention.

She wanted to laugh at the ridiculousness of what she felt. Unfortunately she had already learned that being in love left little room for lighthearted self-mockery. Intellectually, she recognized that she was overdramatizing her situation. Emotionally, she wondered how a person could feel anything as intense as what she felt for Alec and survive. Through the obscuring haze of her emotions, she felt someone touch her arm. She turned around and realized, belatedly, that Sam was talking to her.

"Well, are you surprised, Caitlin?"

She had absolutely no idea what he was talking about. "Should I be?" she asked.

"You were the one who told me Jodie would never be talked out of going to Africa."

Caitlin's heart seemed to explode in a flash of blinding, crippling pain. *This is how it felt to have all your hopes dashed in one swift, crushing blow,* she thought. She sensed everyone watching her, sensed an undercurrent of speculation, and pride forced her to gather her wits to try to respond normally. She cleared her throat several times before she could speak. "You must be very happy, Sam."

He snorted. "I suppose Mexico is a bit closer at least. Dot and I can visit her at Easter, I guess."

"Mexico?" she blurted out, staring first at Jodie and then at Alec. "You're going to move to Mexico?"

"Not me," Alec said shortly. "Jodie."

Damping down a leap of wild hope, Caitlin realized she had daydreamed through a very important piece of conversation. Unfortunately, she couldn't ask too many questions without revealing that she'd heard nothing anybody had said since Alec rang the doorbell.

"What made you decide on Mexico?" she asked Jodie, hoping the question was at least marginally appropriate.

"Alec persuaded me." Jodie hooked her arm through Alec's and looked up at him with an adoring gaze. "He put me in touch with a friend of his who runs a special research lab in Monterey, which is the second largest city in Mexico. The lab runs field projects all over the country, and they have connections to Stanford University, so I'll be able to get in some really important on-site research and work toward my doctorate at the same time.''

"That's really great," Caitlin said. She tried not to show the relief that was washing over her in huge, ecstatic waves.

Alec isn't going to marry Jodie.

She forced her best imitation of a casual grin. "I guess that means I've blown my chance for making vice president of Services Unlimited before Christmas. You were my last hope as far as marrying off Alec was concerned."

"I should think we'd have women lined up on the sidewalk begging for a date," Sam said, casting her a sly sideways glance.

"Thanks for the vote of support," Alec said. "You know, Caity, there's always Helen. Somehow, in my heart of hearts, I'm convinced Helen is the right woman for me. Maybe it's the thought of her wonderful red hair. I've always been very partial to redheads. Do you think you could arrange a date for us?"

"Absolutely not," Caitlin said. "I'm sure you wouldn't suit each other at all."

"Why not? She sounds exactly like the woman I'm looking for."

"Two days ago, you were crazy about Jodie and convinced that Helen's career was too demanding! What in the world has gotten into you, Alec?"

Dot, Jodie, Sam and Alec all spoke at once. Alec finally cut through the babble of explanations. "I think Helen would agree to marry me if she'd only give me a chance to discuss our future prospects rationally."

"You'd never heard of her until two days ago!" Caitlin protested, thoroughly infuriated by Alec's cavalier attitude and even more infuriated by his resurrection of the nonexistent Helen.

"What's time got to do with romance?" he asked vaguely. "Helen meets all of my requirements."

"It's absolutely ridiculous to think you can choose a wife just by matching some woman to a prepackaged list of specifications, like selecting curtains for the bathroom. 'Must be blue, no ruffles, preferably machine washable.'"

Sam laughed, but Alec looked at her, his eyes suddenly dark and intense. "I'll cut you a deal, Caity. Bring Helen to my apartment tonight, and I guarantee you'll be astonished at the results. Don't you want to get your vice presidency by Christmas?"

Caitlin should have known better than to set her feet further on the slippery slope of deception, but her mouth gave the fateful agreement before her brain had the sense to veto it. "You're on," she said. "You want Helen, you've got her. Nine o'clock tonight at your apartment."

"Hey, wait a minute," Dot protested. "No woman is going to agree to a first meeting in a strange man's apartment."

"Don't worry about it," Alec said. "Caitlin will be there to reassure her that I don't bite, won't you?"

"I'll be there," Caitlin said. "You can count on it."

CHAPTER ELEVEN

CAITLIN SMOOTHED the palms of her hands over her jeans and waited for the butterflies in her stomach to stop swarming. They failed to oblige. Tonight, even her stomach refused to cooperate and make life a little easier.

The elevator was paneled with smoked glass, and she stared at her murky reflection in the vain hope that she would miraculously have become ten times more attractive during the short car ride from her apartment to Alec's. Unfortunately, no fairy godmother had chosen to wave a magic wand. She looked pretty much the way she always looked. Probably, she thought despairingly, pretty much the way she'd looked when she was sixteen, and Alec, on the banks of the fishing pond, had tactfully rejected the offer of her overflowing teenage heart.

She scowled at her reflection, wondering why in the world she'd decided to wear jeans, which were calculated to create exactly the wrong sort of juvenile image. The elevator stopped, and she stepped out onto the fourteenth floor, Alec's floor, telling herself it was too late to worry about what she was wearing.

She had changed her outfit literally a dozen times before settling on jeans and a shirt of turquoise silk, topped by a leather jacket. Not the sort of clothes to set a man's libido racing into overdrive, but since Alec was likely to throw her out the moment she admitted the truth about Helen, it had seemed a bit ridiculous to come obviously dressed for seduction.

Her breath caught in her throat, and her finger paused smack dab over Alec's doorbell. *Dressed for seduction.* At last she'd admitted the truth, at least to herself. Using Helen as an excuse, she had come here tonight to seduce Alec, to gamble everything on a final, high-stakes throw.

She didn't have much confidence in her powers as a seductress—her experience was far too limited—but she tried to reassure herself with the thought that Alec already liked her, so maybe it wouldn't take much to persuade him that he could make a happy marriage with her. Caitlin tried to keep her level of hope high, since right now hope was about all she had. Squaring her shoulders, she pressed the doorbell before her courage could desert her.

Alec opened the door. "Hi, Caity." He brushed her cheek in the sort of friendly greeting he had given her a thousand times before. She jumped as if he'd inserted red-hot needles under her thumbnails.

"Something wrong?" Alec inquired politely.

"Oh, n-no, nothing. I'm fine." *Great,* she told herself sarcastically. *You're going to make a wonderful seductress if you leap like a gazelle every time he comes within two feet of you.*

For a fleeting moment she thought she saw laughter in Alec's eyes, then the laughter vanished and he stepped out into the corridor, looking up and down and all around her. "Where's Helen?" he asked. "Did she get called away again, or was she just unwilling to meet me?"

"It's, um, a long story," Caitlin said. "Could I . . . could I come in, Alec?"

"Of course. My pleasure." He stepped back, the picture of a courteous host, and gestured for her to precede him into the living room.

"Let me take your jacket," he said, reaching up and helping her to slip it off without waiting for her agreement. His hands slid slowly down her arms, rubbing the silk of her blouse against her skin. He was standing so close behind her she could feel the whisper of his breath against her neck. Caitlin closed her eyes as her nerve endings went haywire.

"Is something the matter?" Alec murmured, his touch suddenly turning brisk. "You seem to be covered in goose bumps. Shall I turn up the heat?"

She catapulted out of his arms. "Oh, no, no thanks. I'm just fine. Perfectly fine."

He tossed her jacket over a chair. "Could I get you some coffee? A few Belgian chocolates for old times sake? I still have some of your private supply in the freezer."

"N-no. No, thank you." *Way to go, Caitlin. This is the sort of witty, sparkling dialogue that would seduce any man.* Angry with her gaucheness, she seized the dregs of her courage and swung around to face him. "We need to talk about Helen."

Alec smiled, the sort of predatory smile that had sent chills down the spines of innumerable witnesses for the prosecution. Caitlin's spine tingled, proving it was equally vulnerable. "Believe me, Caity, I'm looking forward to hearing everything you have to say." He tossed another log onto the fire. "Why don't you sit down and get comfortable before you start?"

Caitlin lowered herself onto the extreme edge of the sofa, feeling about as relaxed as a high-wire acrobat about to perform a triple-turn jump without a safety net. "Nice fire," she managed. "Is it your first of the season?"

"Yes, it is. And before you ask, the wood is cherry, and my supplier brings it in from Maryland."

"The wood smells wonderful. You must...you must give me his name."

"I'll do that. Later, if you still want it. Now, tell me about Helen." Alec sat down on the sofa next to her, so close she could feel the heat of his body, so close she smelled the subtle tang of his cologne with every breath she drew. Alec leaned back against the sofa cushions, and the shifting of his weight inevitably caused her to tumble back with him. Her head ended up resting on the crook of his shoulder, and she squirmed hastily away.

Alec waited until she had repositioned herself in her former awkward position at the edge of the sofa. "Feeling better now?"

"M-much better, thanks."

"Personally, I'm feeling frustrated. I've spent most of the afternoon fantasizing about the way this evening might end. And it certainly wasn't with you perched on the edge of your seat looking as if someone had shoved a steel rod down your back."

Caitlin's precarious hold on her self-control snapped, and she jumped up. "Then you've fantasized in vain," she said crossly. "Not just for tonight, but forever. There *is* no Helen, there *was* no Helen, and there never *will* be a Helen. I invented her—she doesn't exist!"

Alec jumped up, too. "I can't believe it!" he said, sounding astonished, which Caitlin supposed wasn't unreasonable. And yet, his astonishment didn't ring true. She had the peculiar impression that in reality he wasn't even marginally surprised. He reached out and put his hands on her shoulders, his gaze suddenly very intent. "Why did you invent her, Caity? It seems like a curious thing to do, especially for you."

She told him half the truth. "At the time, you seemed set to marry Jodie Bergen, and I didn't think you were at all suited to each other."

Alec grinned. "Mama Maria doesn't agree. She said we were a perfect couple, and you know she claims to have second sight."

"She obviously needs an eye examination. She said we were a perfect couple, too. Remember?"

He crooked his finger under her chin and tilted her face upward. "You're right. I guess that ought to warn me not to trust Mama Maria's judgments."

"Her pizza's more reliable than her folk wisdom," Caitlin said, hoping Alec wouldn't notice that she was perilously close to tears. "I can't believe you took Jodie to Mama Maria's," she wailed. "That's our special place."

He brushed his thumb over her lips, his touch gentle. "Is it?" he said huskily. "I didn't realize you felt so possessive about where I take my dates to eat pizza."

She swayed toward him. His head inched fractionally lower. "Choosing pizza toppings is a very intimate process," she whispered. "It tells you a lot about a person."

"Like kissing," he said, and closed the tiny gap between their mouths. "Like making love."

She knew from previous experience exactly what would happen the moment their lips touched. Sure enough, the fireworks exploded, the brass band began to play, her heart melted, her soul caught on fire. But none of the clichés really expressed the way she felt. She'd come home, Caitlin realized. With Alec's arms holding her, she felt as close to perfect happiness as she was likely to find here on earth.

When their kiss finally ended, he cupped her face in his hands and looked down at her, his eyes dark with tenderness. "It's time for us to stop playing games," he said softly. "No more lies, no more half-truths, no more mythical Helens, no more pretending I'm interested in little girls like Jodie Bergen. Are you ready to stop running, Caity?"

She laughed shakily. "I can't run. My legs have turned to jelly."

"Great. But maybe I'd better kiss you one more time just to make sure." He captured her mouth again, covering her lips in a passionate, seeking kiss, miraculously tempered by sweetness. Caitlin closed her eyes and let the desire build slowly, fiercely, inside her.

"Caity." This time his voice was huskier. "Caity, I want to make love to you. Come to bed with me."

"Yes," she said, the last of her doubts vanishing in a blaze of fierce longing. "Alec, I love you so much."

His laughter held more than a hint of pain. "I've been waiting for years to hear you say that."

"You have? Does that mean you love me, too?"

He held her tight against his body. "Let me show you how much," he murmured, and took her hand to lead her into the bedroom.

LATER, SNUGLY WRAPPED in one of Alec's robes, Caitlin curled up in his lap in front of the fire. Resting her head on his shoulder, she sipped contentedly at a cup of fresh-brewed coffee.

Alec twined his hands around hers. The warmth from the cup seeped through their fingers. "Marry me?" he asked.

She smiled radiantly. "Yes, please."

"Does December the fifth sound like a good day? In Hapsburg, Ohio, with both our families present in full force?"

"I'd like that a lot." She gazed at him, replete with love, drowsy with happiness. "Do you think our families will be pleased?"

He laughed. "Only you could ask that question, Caity, my love. Our families have been trying to arrange this wedding for the past ten years at least. My mother finally got desperate and told me she was going to book the church and the Veterans' Hall for the reception, so I'd darn well better produce you as the bride!"

"She did?" Caitlin went pink with pleasure. "You mean you're not just marrying me because you've decided it's time to settle down? You really do love me?"

"Caity, my beloved idiot, I've loved you passionately, insanely and totally for years. Probably ever since you were sixteen and came to me by the fishing pond. Even then, you had the most kissable mouth I'd ever seen."

"Then what did you mean with all that nonsense about hiring Services Unlimited to find you a suitable bride?"

"I wouldn't call it nonsense, since it seems to have succeeded in capturing your attention at last. I can't claim credit for the idea, though. My mother suggested it to me, and I decided I had nothing to lose."

"You certainly grabbed my attention. I was furious when you casually announced that you'd decided to get married. It took me about a week to realize why I was so angry. I wanted you for myself.''

"I kept trying to tell you how I felt, but you wouldn't listen. You just weren't ready to make a commitment, and I was terrified of scaring you off for good. Every time I tried to change the basis of our relationship, you ran a hundred miles in the opposite direction."

"It's taken me a while to realize that marriage to you doesn't mean total loss of my identity." She sighed. "You know, we'll have to do some hard thinking about juggling our careers. However much I love you, I'm not ready to give up my job. I'm just not the domestic type, Alec."

"I wouldn't want you to change." He took her hand and brought it to his cheek. "We'll make it work, Caity, don't worry."

She knew there would be problems ahead, particularly when they had children, but she also knew that the rewards of marriage to Alec were going to make those problems seem trivial by comparison. She leaned forward and kissed him. "Yes," she said. "We'll make it work."

The answering kiss he gave her was so intense it was a long time before either of them had breath or energy for any more conversation. Several minutes passed before she stirred in his arms. "What about that woman your mother told me you wanted to marry? I think I'm jealous. You never told me her name."

He kissed her tenderly on the nose. "Idiot," he said lovingly. "That woman was you. My mother was trying to find out how you felt about me."

"You could have asked me yourself."

"And sent you fleeing? You weren't ready to get married, Caity. It's taken you a long time to realize that marriage isn't a trap, but a gateway."

"I got engaged to David," she protested.

"Because he was safe," Alec said. "I was terrified you might drift into marriage with him, but in my heart of hearts, I knew the two of you were never going to follow through on your commitment. David was kind, he was decent, and you didn't care two cents for him. That's why it felt safe for you to get engaged."

"Are you going to insist on psychoanalyzing me once we're married?"

He kissed her tenderly. "Only when I can't think of anything better to do." He straightened and poured her more coffee from the pot heating by the hearth. She smiled at him over the rim of the cup. "Mmm...what a fabulous man you are. You do realize I'm only marrying you for your coffee, don't you?"

"Don't forget my chocolates. Although I can't help thinking my superb skills in the bedroom must have something to do with your change of heart."

She pretended to consider. "No," she said at last. "It's definitely the coffee."

"Liar." He leaned over and expertly removed the cup from her fingers. Then he trailed tantalizing kisses over her cheeks and the hollows of her throat, while his hands wrought magic over the rest of her body. She arched toward him, immediately responsive, but he simply smiled, tormenting her with his refusal to give her the deeper, more satisfying kisses she craved. His lips hovered a breath away from hers.

"You can't win this game, Caity," he murmured. "Now, let's try again. Why did you agree to marry me?"

"For—your—coffee."

His hands brushed over the swell of her breast. His eyes danced with laughter—and desire. "Why are you marrying me?"

"Because I love you, you arrogant beast!"

"Amazing! That's the very same reason I'm marrying you."

"Prove it to me," she whispered.

He did.

EVEN THE OLD-TIMERS agreed that Hapsburg, Ohio, had never seen a more splendid wedding than that of Caitlin Elizabeth Howard and Alec Harrison Woodward. The locals were delighted that two of their own had shown the good sense to fall in love with each other, and they were forgiven for having taken so long to make up their minds.

The bride, looking ethereal in ivory satin, was declared the prettiest of the decade, and the groom—whose successful defense of Leon Mancuso had made news headlines across the country—looked both handsome and passionately in love. The maid of honor, Mrs. Sam Bergen, was pronounced too old for the role, but most guests conceded she looked more than okay in a gown of deep rose silk, which someone declared had been her own wedding dress.

If Hapsburg found the maid-of-honor situation rather odd and "big city," the flower girls met with unstinted approval, and the ring bearers, Matt and Zach, were considered amazingly well behaved. Both little boys refrained from throwing up until more than halfway through the reception, which everyone agreed was a minor miracle given the quantity of wedding cake they consumed.

Hapsburg wasn't impressed by the parade of Washington bigwigs who ventured into the Midwest hinterland for the wedding—it took more than a tuxedo and a fancy accent to impress a Hapsburgian—but the Grand Gourmet caterers were acknowledged to have done a terrific job with the buffet dinner, and the band from Cleveland was rated hot stuff. All in all, the Howards and the Woodwards had put on a darn good show, worthy of third-generation natives. The townfolk were content.

IN THEIR HOTEL SUITE in the Bahamas, Alec took Caitlin into his arms with a sigh of profound relief. "Alone at last. Would you care for some champagne, Mrs. Woodward?"

"Mmm. Yes, please." She took the flute of champagne and followed him out onto the balcony overlooking the ocean. She felt a familiar thrill of pleasure as his arms closed around her waist, drawing her back against his body. Looking out across the endless vista of dark ocean, it seemed that her life shimmered ahead of her, dazzling with new possibilities and fresh horizons. A tropical breeze blew off the sea, warm, perfumed and gently caressing, the perfect benediction at the end of a perfect day. Caitlin wished she could capture her feelings at this moment and store them forever.

Alec's voice rippled over her, low, husky and full of promise. "I love you, Caity."

She turned in his arms. "I love you, too." She thought back over the day just ended. "I think everything went off well, don't you? Our families were ecstatic and our friends had a good time."

"Everything went wonderfully. Maybe even too well. From the gleam in my mother's eyes, I think we've just whetted her appetite."

"How so?"

"A few minutes before we left, I heard her discussing baby showers with you mother. And she wasn't talking about Merry."

Caitlin laughed, but her body flushed with the heat of sudden longing. "How much time to you think we have before they begin pressuring us to start a family?"

"They won't want to rush us." Alec chuckled. "I reckon we might have a month after we get back from our honeymoon before they start dropping hints. Six weeks if we're extra lucky."

Caitlin realized that the prospect of being pregnant with Alec's child no longer seemed confining or limiting, but the fulfillment of her most cherished dream. She lifted her hand and touched his hair where the breeze blew if onto his forehead. "I'd like to get a head start on the project," she said softly. "How about you?"

He captured her hand and pressed a long, hard kiss into the palm. "Mrs. Woodward, I can hardly wait."

Let

HARLEQUIN ROMANCE®

take you

BACK TO THE RANCH

Come to the Lucky Horseshoe Ranch, near Pepper, Texas!

Meet Cody Bailman—cattle rancher, single father and Texan—and Sherry Waterman, a nurse-midwife who's new to town.

Read LONE STAR LOVIN' by Debbie Macomber, July's Back to the Ranch title!

Available wherever Harlequin Books are sold.

OFFICIAL RULES • MILLION DOLLAR MATCH 3 SWEEPSTAKES
NO PURCHASE OR OBLIGATION NECESSARY TO ENTER

To enter, follow the directions published. **ALTERNATE MEANS OF ENTRY:** Hand print your name and address on a 3"×5" card and mail to either: Harlequin "Match 3," 3010 Walden Ave., P.O. Box 1867, Buffalo, NY 14269-1867 or Harlequin "Match 3," P.O. Box 609, Fort Erie, Ontario L2A 5X3, and we will assign your Sweepstakes numbers. (Limit: one entry per envelope.) For eligibility, entries must be received no later than March 31, 1994. No responsibility is assumed for lost, late or misdirected entries.

Upon receipt of entry, Sweepstakes numbers will be assigned. To determine winners, Sweepstakes numbers will be compared against a list of randomly preselected prizewinning numbers. In the event all prizes are not claimed via the return of prizewinning numbers, random drawings will be held from among all other entries received to award unclaimed prizes.

Prizewinners will be determined no later than May 30, 1994. Selection of winning numbers and random drawings are under the supervision of D.L. Blair, Inc., an independent judging organization, whose decisions are final. One prize to a family or organization. No substitution will be made for any prize, except as offered. Taxes and duties on all prizes are the sole responsibility of winners. Winners will be notified by mail. Chances of winning are determined by the number of entries distributed and received.

Sweepstakes open to persons 18 years of age or older, except employees and immediate family members of Torstar Corporation, D.L. Blair, Inc., their affiliates, subsidiaries and all other agencies, entities and persons connected with the use, marketing or conduct of this Sweepstakes. All applicable laws and regulations apply. Sweepstakes offer void wherever prohibited by law. Any litigation within the province of Quebec respecting the conduct and awarding of a prize in this Sweepstakes must be submitted to the Régies des Loteries et Courses du Quebec. In order to win a prize, residents of Canada will be required to correctly answer a time-limited arithmetical skill-testing question. Values of all prizes are in U.S. currency.

Winners of major prizes will be obligated to sign and return an affidavit of eligibility and release of liability within 30 days of notification. In the event of non-compliance within this time period, prize may be awarded to an alternate winner. Any prize or prize notification returned as undeliverable will result in the awarding of that prize to an alternate winner. By acceptance of their prize, winners consent to use of their names, photographs or other likenesses for purposes of advertising, trade and promotion on behalf of Torstar Corporation without further compensation, unless prohibited by law.

This Sweepstakes is presented by Torstar Corporation, its subsidiaries and affiliates in conjunction with book, merchandise and/or product offerings. Prizes are as follows: Grand Prize—$1,000,000 (payable at $33,333.33 a year for 30 years). First through Sixth Prizes may be presented in different creative executions, each with the following appproximate values: First Prize—$35,000; Second Prize—$10,000; 2 Third Prizes—$5,000 each; 5 Fourth Prizes—$1,000 each; 10 Fifth Prizes—$250 each; 1,000 Sixth Prizes—$100 each. Prizewinners will have the opportunity of selecting any prize offered for that level. A travel-prize option, if offered and selected by winner, must be completed within 12 months of selection and is subject to hotel and flight accommodations availability. Torstar Corporation may present this Sweepstakes utilizing names other than Million Dollar Sweepstakes. For a current list of all prize options offered within prize levels and all names the Sweepstakes may utilize, send a self-addressed, stamped envelope (WA residents need not affix return postage) to: Million Dollar Sweepstakes Prize Options/Names, P.O. Box 4710, Blair, NE 68009.

The Extra Bonus Prize will be awarded in a random drawing to be conducted no later than May 30, 1994 from among all entries received. To qualify, entries must be received by March 31, 1994 and comply with published directions. No purchase necessary. For complete rules, send a self-addressed, stamped envelope (WA residents need not affix return postage) to: Extra Bonus Prize Rules, P.O. Box 4600, Blair, NE 68009.

For a list of prizewinners (available after July 31, 1994) send a separate, stamped, self-addressed envelope to: Million Dollar Sweepstakes Winners, P.O. Box 4728, Blair, NE 68009.

Relive the romance...
Harlequin and Silhouette are proud to present

by Request

A program of collections of three complete novels by the most requested authors with the most requested themes. Be sure to look for one volume each month with three complete novels by top name authors.

In June: **NINE MONTHS** Penny Jordan
Stella Cameron
Janice Kaiser

Three women pregnant and alone. But a lot can happen in nine months!

In July: **DADDY'S HOME** Kristin James
Naomi Horton
Mary Lynn Baxter

Daddy's Home...and his presence is long overdue!

In August: **FORGOTTEN PAST** Barbara Kaye
Pamela Browning
Nancy Martin

Do you dare to create a future if you've forgotten the past?

Available at your favorite retail outlet.

HARLEQUIN® *Silhouette*

Discover the glorious triumph of three
extraordinary couples fueled by a powerful
passion to defy the past in

*Lingering
Shadows*

The dramatic story of six fascinating men and
women who find the strength to step out of the
shadows and into the light of a passionate future.

Linked by relentless ambition and by desire, each
must confront private demons in a riveting struggle
for power. Together they must find the strength to
emerge from the lingering shadows of the past, into
the dawning promise of the future.

Look for this powerful new blockbuster by *New
York Times* bestselling author

PENNY
JORDAN

Available in August at your favorite retail outlet.

THREE UNFORGETTABLE HEROINES
THREE AWARD-WINNING AUTHORS

Untamed

MAVERICK HEARTS

A unique collection of historical short stories that
capture the spirit of America's last frontier.

HEATHER GRAHAM POZZESSERE—over 10 million copies
of her books in print worldwide
Lonesome Rider—The story of an Eastern widow and the
renegade half-breed who becomes her protector.

PATRICIA POTTER—an author whose books are consistently
Waldenbooks bestsellers
Against the Wind—Two people, battered by heartache, prove
that love can heal all.

JOAN JOHNSTON—award-winning Western historical author
with 17 books to her credit
One Simple Wish—A woman with a past discovers that
dreams really do come true.

Join us for an exciting journey West with
UNTAMED
Available in July, wherever Harlequin books are sold.